THE
FLOWERING

THE

FLOWERING

The

Flowering

by

Alison Littlewood

BLACK SHUCK
SHADOWS

Black Shuck Books
www.BlackShuckBooks.co.uk

Versions of the following stories first appeared as follows:
'The Zoetrope' in *The Dark* #61 (2020)
'The Marvellous Talking Machine' in *Phantoms* (Titan Books, 2018)
'Meet Me at the Frost Fair' in *A Midwinter Entertainment* (Egaeus Press, 2016)
'The Ballad Box' in *Murder Ballads* (Egaeus Press, 2017)
'The Winter Tree' as a chapbook (White Noise Press, 2016)

Cover design & internal layout © WHITEspace 2022
www.white-space.uk

First published in the UK by Black Shuck Books, 2022

978-1-913038-96-0

The Zoetrope

My mother gave me the zoetrope on my birthday and it was my favourite possession, not so much for its own sake or even the magic it held within, but because it was something we shared. Her gift, a hollow cylinder of carved wood, came with a set of various images on strips of paper. Mother placed the zoetrope on its stand, positioned one of the strips inside the drum and set it spinning. At first, it seemed unremarkable; I frowned at the tick-ticking it made, not understanding, until she bent and looked through one of the slits in the circumference, showing me what to do.

I still remember, quite clearly, what I saw through the narrow gap – not a sequence of simple pictures as they had appeared a moment ago, but a line of galloping horses, throwing out their legs in a smooth motion, never catching one another but never ceasing in their running. She peeked at me over the top of the drum and made it spin more rapidly; the horses' legs became a blur as they increased their pace.

'This was originally called a daedalum,' she said. 'Now we take its name from the Greek – *zoe* for life and *tropos* for turning. And so, Frances, the zoetrope is a wheel of life. It always goes back to the beginning – you see?'

I did see. The illusion of movement had its limit: the sequence was short and simple and repetitive and so were the others in the box, but still we laughed over the sight of a whale surfacing from the sea, a ballerina performing her grand-jetés, a Jack-in-the-box leaping forth, a ball endlessly passing through a hoop.

Then my mother slotted the next strip into the cylinder and we watched a man and a woman waltzing together. It did not matter what speed the wheel spun; they were always in time, always together, always close.

I shifted my gaze from the whirling image of the couple, whom it was easy to imagine being very much in love, and focused instead upon my mother's eye, peering through the opposite slit; at the tear that was brimming there, motionless, not quite ready to fall.

After that came yet more magic, for new images appeared, ones that my mother began to create herself. It became a tradition for her to leave the papers in my room for me to discover, to fit them into the cylinder and view them without her saying a word.

The first time it happened, I recognised her style in the neat pencil and watercolour pictures, but I tried not to look at them too closely as I placed the band of paper in the drum. Instead, I set it spinning and bent to look through the slits.

The image was of a girl, clasping a rosebud to her breast. As I watched, it opened, flowering in shades of crimson. Though the movement was imperfect, I did not know how my mother had made it appear so lifelike; perhaps it was because she had breathed her love into it. The image seemed almost to hover in the air, a little in front of the spinning strip of paper. The girl depicted there was me.

Her second creation also pictured me, and this time I was dancing, though I had no partner. I spun the drum first one way and then the other, quickly and then slower. She had the mastered the illusion of movement even better this time, though my gaze was fixed on the look of perfect happiness on my face.

Softly, the door opened behind me and I heard the rustle of my mother's skirts. She walked in, bent and peered through the opposite side of the drum.

I do not believe she ever took any real pleasure in her beautifully made images, not for their own sake. She did not even appear to look at them. Instead she looked through the device, fixing on me; at the expression of wonder in my eye.

I imagined dancing like the version of myself she had envisaged, and I couldn't. For the images seemed to suggest more than a simple dance; they seemed rather to represent life itself – the wheel of life.

Of course, the converse of life was death, but she did not approach that in her drawings, not then. Soon after, my father sent me away to finishing school. By the time I was brought home again, my mother was already gone.

~

I learned from a library book, at school, why the zoetrope was originally named the daedalum. I had assumed it was simply because the mythical Daedalus was a craftsman and inventor, though I also knew his creations did not always go aright. He constructed the Minotaur's labyrinth, containing the beast, but also making it almost impossible to slay. Daedalus was locked in a tower for his pains, to preserve the secret of the maze. To escape, he constructed wings for himself and his son, Icarus – who flew too close to the sun, melting the wax that fixed his feathers in place, and fell from his heights to his doom.

Now I learned that Daedalus was also renowned for carving figures that were so very lifelike, they possessed the gift of self-motion. Indeed, his statues would have walked away and escaped, were it not for the chains that bound them to the wall.

My father, whom I had not seen in over a year, sent the maid, Nella, to meet my train when I returned home. She greeted me shyly; had I really changed so much? She hailed a hansom cab and we crammed into it along with my bag, so that it was something of a relief when I found myself in my room, alone once more.

I paced for a while, touching the familiar objects as if to assure myself they were still there: the marble topped wash-stand, the faded blue hangings of my bed, and yes, the zoetrope, standing on its cabinet. Then I left the room and went to the stairs down which my mother had fallen.

I descended the steps slowly and deliberately, not for fear of falling, but to contemplate each one. Was this wooden edge the one that had caused such terrible injuries? Had this riser struck the final blow – or this?

When I reached the bottom, I had learned nothing. I only felt that the stairs seemed smaller than they once had, as did the whole silent house. I wished I could sense what had happened to her, read the past hanging in the air all about me, but it was beyond my reach.

I returned to my room and stood in front of the zoetrope. It was just as it had always been, not a trace of dust to signal the passage of time. I bent to one of the viewing slits, half expecting to see my mother's eye looking back at me from the opposite side. What expression would it reveal? But the drum was innocent of pictures; the wheel of life was empty.

I searched out the strips of paper with their sequences of images and made my choice – not one of those my mother had made for me, since I could not bear to look at those, not yet. Instead I took up the printed ones that came with the toy, fitted one into the drum and turned it. As it spun, the familiar ticking began, the sound of time passing, and the faint trace of my mother's perfume rose into the air, the lavender-water she always wore. I stared down at the man and woman performing their waltz, like a child peeking through a gap in a doorway to spy upon a longed-for ball. And I frowned, for it was not quite as I remembered it.

The man certainly seemed to move as he always had, but his figure was surely a little more stout – and it came to me, in a shock, that he resembled my father. I told myself it could not be so, however, for my father preferred to be clean shaven, whereas the dancer within was adorned with a tidy little moustache. The woman, though – a chill shuddered through me at the sight of her, for she was my mother to the life, although she wore a peculiar expression; her eyes were wide as if with fear, and her movements were jerky, not quite in time with her husband's. She lagged – indeed, he almost appeared to be dragging her about, hurling her in endless circles while she teetered on the verge of falling to the floor.

I started away from the ticking drum, rubbing my eyes. It could not have changed; it wasn't possible. The dancing man must always have looked like my father, his partner resembling any lady with chestnut hair. Perhaps it was only that I had changed, and the difference lay in the way I viewed it.

But I could think on it no further, for Nella tapped on my door and informed me that my father had summoned me, that he required me to take my mother's place and pour his tea. For an instant I thought of a girl with a rose blossoming in her hands, a child becoming a woman, stepping into another's place; and I heard the echo of my mother's voice.

It always goes back to the beginning – you see?

I suddenly pictured all the days stretching in front of me, doing exactly the same things – ensuring his cup was full, endlessly sewing some useless frippery, donning my finest gown for his acquaintances. And it struck me: is that what I was now – what my mother had been? Were we nothing but fine figures chained to a wall, perfectly carved but never to speak, never to move without his volition, never to leave? Did we exist only to be seen and admired like a statue, or a flower blossoming in a closed room – our only movement nothing but an endless circle, the same pre-ordained patterns repeating themselves hour after hour, and always returning to the beginning again?

~

While the gentlemen spoke of business, I poured tea, passed bread and butter, and made low murmuring replies to any polite remarks they sent in my direction. The acquaintance had some mutual interest in trade and was somewhat unprepossessing, with loose, florid cheeks that wobbled as he spoke and full, moist lips. It was my father's appearance which most commanded my attention, however, for I could not help but wonder when he had decided to cultivate his neat little moustache.

I had endeavoured to cover my surprise at the sight of it when we were reunited. He had smiled and clasped my hand before standing back to nod approvingly at my appearance, which he declared much improved. His friend peered at me likewise before making some attempt at a gallant remark and I tried not to squirm under his observation.

Now, seated at the table, I gathered myself to examine the changes in my father more minutely. The moustache was not the only change in him; his figure was perhaps a little more stout – though, oddly, his face seemed if anything rather gaunt. His cheeks had sunk inward and his forehead was lined, as if some great concern hung over him, or perhaps sorrow; I supposed at my mother's death.

It was odd sitting there trying to make him out, as if he were a stranger. But then, he had always been a rather remote figure to me; someone whose movements were familiar but with whom I had little connection, as if he moved in an entirely different circle, one that rarely touched upon mine.

I remembered the image dancing within the zoetrope and frowned. Had the little figure always worn a moustache, and I had simply forgotten it? Or had my mother in some whimsical moment re-drawn the dancers and replaced the strip? If she had, her ability to mimic the style of the printed versions was admirable – but she had never done such a thing before. Why should she? Her own paintings held so much more character; so much more life.

My mind whirled with images, changing as they spun, each being replaced by things that looked alike and yet were so very different, while I made my automatic responses to my father and his guest. It came as a relief when I was able to return to my room, though my confusion did not fade when I saw what awaited me there.

There was a strip of paper lying on my bed. I saw at once that it bore a sequence of images, not printed but painted. They were in my mother's style and for a moment I turned, half expecting to see her standing in the doorway.

Of course, it was empty. I closed the door and picked up the paper, resisting the urge to look at it more closely. I wished to view the images as she would have intended; dancing, not fixed in place and lifeless. I held my breath as I fitted them into the cylinder and set it spinning, telling myself I must have inadvertently left this strip out of the box, that I would see nothing new, nothing I had not already seen countless times.

But it was not anything I had seen before. This was new, and I saw at once that my mother was in it, and my father, and me. My father had not yet grown his moustache, and it was plain to see how anger curled his lip as he carried out his action – thrusting me from the door whilst my mother clung to his frock-coat, her features distorted by dismay.

I slowed the movement, focusing on my own face. The sorrowful glance I cast at my mother brought fresh tears; I remembered it so well. It was the last time I would ever see her.

I had not been ejected from the house in quite such a manner, of course. I had left quietly, obedient to my father's wish, though I had known my mother did not share it. She tried to ease the way for me, though, even echoing his words; telling me the school would teach me to conduct myself in the most seemly fashion, that it would be the making of me.

I always knew they were his words, not her own, even before the scene was laid out before me so very plainly in the zoetrope. My mother must have painted this after I left, then decided out of loyalty to her husband that she would not give it to me. I supposed Nella must have found it among her things and placed it by the toy for which it was intended.

Still, I could not help but feel that the moment had been chosen somehow, that here was a message, sent to me by my mother's hand; that she had found a way to show me this sign of her love.

~

That evening I sat with my father in the drawing room, sewing a sampler while he read his newspaper. I cast glances in his direction now and then, though I do not believe he once looked at me. I remembered how assiduous he had been in observing my appearance when his friend was present and it occurred to me, with a numbing chill, that he meant for me to marry the man. I remembered those moist red lips and shuddered.

I escaped for the evening as soon as I could, pleading tiredness, so overcome that when I first saw the paper left on the cabinet, I did not realise what it was.

When I placed the new sequence of images into the zoetrope, however, and set it spinning, I saw my father again, and my mother too, but I could not clearly see her face. Her chestnut hair had come unpinned, was hanging loose in unruly curls in a way I had never seen it in life. Through the strands, however, I thought I could make out the gleam of tears.

They were sitting in the drawing room with tea laid out before them. My mother was leaning across the table but instead of pouring the tea she kept sweeping her hand across it all, overturning the cups. I recognised the gold rims and little blue flowers of her wedding china.

As ever, the motion had its limit. The cups returned to their place. She swept her arm; they were scattered again, over and over, always the same, while my father started from his seat, raising his fist.

His blow never fell, but I kept waiting for it, unable to tear my gaze away. I wished I could climb inside the zoetrope and enter that room, to see what had come before, what came after. Instead I stopped it spinning and snatched the paper, holding it up before the lamp. Could my mother truly have painted this? Had my parents ever behaved in such a way? I had always surmised they were not as some spouses are, not always spinning through life in a perfect waltz. There had been disagreements, bitter voices overheard from closed rooms, so low I could never make out the words, but I thought they had always done their duty by one another.

Had my father struck my mother? Was this the true reason I had been sent away?

My consternation was such that I did not for a time begin to wonder how these images came to be in my room. My mother could surely never have painted them. And the maid, Nella, could not have brought them: for it was her half day, and it was many hours since she had left the house.

I took a steadying breath, and realised something else; the air was laced with the scent of my mother's lavender water, still hanging in the air.

~

The next morning I descended the stairs to the kitchen and went to the pantry. I wanted to examine my mother's china – to see if all of it was intact. Nella was busy blacking the range and so I was left alone to turn each cup in my hands, running my fingers over the little blue flowers. My mother had been so fond of them, though now I discovered that two of the lovely gold-rimmed cups were missing and one of the saucers was chipped.

I enquired of Nella what had become of them.

'I'm sure I don't know, Miss Frances,' she replied, looking up so briefly from her task that it was difficult to ascertain if something was hidden in her eyes; some knowledge she did not wish to impart.

'Tell me, Nella, have you happened to come across some pictures painted by my mother? Or rather sequences of pictures, arranged on long strips of paper – did you leave such things in my room?'

She only shook her head, but her expression was so guileless I could not doubt her. Yet she must be lying, for what else could it be? There was no one else in the house and my father certainly would not have given those images to me. He would rather have destroyed them.

I stared at the maid a moment longer before walking from the kitchen. I had no thought of what to do next and found myself going all about the house, standing for a time outside my father's study before ascending the stairs to my mother's bedroom. I pulled open the wardrobe to see that her lovely gowns had gone; there was nothing within but mournful dark jackets and clean white shirts. I could not bear to look at them and rushed from the room, finding myself standing at the top of the stairs, staring down at the polished wood.

They had said that my mother's injuries were dreadful. They forbade me from seeing her in her coffin; they said I could not come home.

'Whatever are you doing there, Frances?'

I raised my head and saw my father standing at the foot of the stairs, his forehead creased more heavily than ever. I had no answer to give him. I did not know how to tell him that I had been seeking my mother's ghost.

~

My father instructed me to compose myself, and I did, for his acquaintance was again called to the house and my presence was required. I stood before my father while he cast his eyes over my appearance and nodded. I tried not to look at his friend as I once again poured tea, passed bread and butter, and made low murmuring replies to any polite remarks they sent in my direction.

Then there came a change of tone in our guest's voice and I caught the tail end of some comment about my father's 'poor dear wife.' I looked up to find that my father's gaze was fixed, not upon his friend, but on me.

I squirmed under his look and could not prevent myself blurting, 'I do so wish I could have returned for her funeral.'

My father was quick to reply. 'A true lady would never have attended such a thing.'

His tone, rather than his words, silenced me. Did he think me forward? Did he imagine that I would be – *should* be – too delicate for such an occasion? I tried to tell myself that he only wanted what was best for me, that he would protect me from distress, and yet I could not help but think there was more; something beneath the surface that I could not see. Perhaps it was only that he did not wish me to conduct myself in a less than seemly fashion, not where others could see.

'The lady of the house must be greatly missed,' said his guest.

My father grimaced. Was it so painful to hear her spoken of? Indeed, he did not reply, only gestured towards me as if to turn the subject. 'My daughter,' he said, 'is the image of her mother at that age.'

'Oh – yes,' replied his guest, and the red tip of his tongue touched his full lips. 'She is a true flower.'

I tried to conceal my disgust. Thankfully, my father said, 'We have much to discuss, Frances. Perhaps you should leave us now.'

For a moment longer I stared at them both, seeing their movements as my father started from his chair and sank into it again, as his friend rattled his teacup with a clumsy hand. I inclined my head and left them.

The first thing I did upon returning to my room was spin the zoetrope on its stand. When

I bent and peered through the slit, I found that the image had changed again, though I had seen this one before. There was the girl – me – holding her rose, the crimson flower just beginning to bloom, and I snapped out a hand and stopped its motion. I spun it the other way, anti-clockwise, and watched the flower shrinking upon itself until it became a bud once more; and yet it always appeared again, as grown and sensuous as ever.

~

At some time I must have closed my eyes and lain down, still dressed, upon my bed. I do not know if I slept or if the images I saw were some waking dream. There was a whirl of repeating motion: my father going to his study; raising a cup to his lips; turning the pages of his newspaper. The sun crossed the sky; the moon shone down; the sun rose. Yet through it all I had the sense of something large and animal following just behind me, stalking me, always keeping pace and yet hidden behind the fragile walls of my prison.

I opened my eyes. Outside the window, day had turned once more to night. And I heard the echo of my mother's voice:

It always goes back to the beginning.

I reached out to clutch the coverlet, perhaps wishing to seize upon reality, and felt the touch of paper under my hand. It came as little surprise to find the strip of painted images that had been placed upon my bed.

I walked to the zoetrope as if in a dream. As I slipped the paper into the drum, I glimpsed flashes of red that danced in the air, the colour almost seeming to cling to my fingertips.

I leaned over the device, somehow finding myself thinking of the Minotaur's labyrinth. That too was a structure that might have had no way in and no way out... yet as the zoetrope began to spin, it became not a maze but a never-ending wheel.

Still I saw, with something like wonder, that it held within its walls a captive bull.

This was no Minotaur, however. It was no huge beast but a figure cast in bronze, and I knew it to be about seven inches high. I had seen it, many times, on the drawing room mantelpiece.

Now my father was holding it in his hand. He was not in the drawing room, however, but at the top of the stairs. My mother was next to him, half kneeling, half crouching, her arms stretched out in entreaty.

I closed my eyes as it happened, but it was no use; I could see it still. Over and again, my father raised the bronze bull and struck down. Blood flew from the wound in her skull. He raised his hand. He struck.

I pictured the waiting stairs. Down, down my mother would fall – but not yet. For now, she still reached for him. Was she pleading or trying to stop his hand? It did not matter. He raised his arm. He struck.

The blood was so brightly crimson. The image was so real I could not doubt its truth. Yet how could my mother have created this image of her own death – of her *murder*? I reached out, stopped the cylinder spinning and snatched the paper from it. I peered at the images and the blood no longer seemed so bright, my mother's expression not so fearful, my father's face less full of hatred. The clarity had faded, but still I knew that these images had been painted by my mother's hand.

She used to tell me that she would love me always. And she did; she had come to me again. She had found a way to visit me, to show me everything she wanted me to know.

But what could I do? I thought of my father somewhere downstairs, going over his papers, sipping brandy, making plans for my marriage. I could do nothing to stop it; the circle was closing upon me.

I sank onto the bed, remaining motionless as my mind spun. Pictures flew past, quicker and quicker, all taking place at once: a crimson flower's sensuous blooming; cups spilled across a table; a woman dragged along in a jerking dance; a bronze bull finding its mark. And I almost fancied that a sound reached my ears – the heavy thud of footfalls, or perhaps hooves, just beyond the walls, which were delicate as paper, too thin to keep them out.

It came to me that the sound was too loud, too close, and I opened my eyes to see my father.

I started away from him, then realised he was not looking at me. He was standing by the old cabinet, leaning over something, and a new sound rose: the tick-ticking of a wheel.

I looked down at my hands. The strip of paper had gone – he must have taken it and fitted it into the cylinder. It was the only way to explain his stillness, the tension that was burning from him.

I knew what it was he saw. And I realised he would think that I was the one who had painted it.

Slowly, he straightened. He seemed so tall, taller than he ever had. He loomed above me, his shoulders broad. He blocked out the light. He seemed not so much stout as muscular, as strong and wordless as a beast, full of thoughts I could not imagine.

He walked from the room and closed the door behind him.

I rose to my feet, staring after him. Where was he at this moment? What was passing through his mind? I knew his secret. Would he return with the bronze bull, the creature ready to do his bidding once more – to silence me?

I looked about the room as if an answer would appear, as if my mother could send some new message. And she must – after all, she had brought me to this juncture. Surely she would not abandon me now – yet there was nothing but silence; the only words that reached me were a memory.

It always goes back to the beginning – you see?

But how could it? The thing my father had done could not be undone. I couldn't unsee it. The beast had escaped; it was in the house. Even now, it might be pacing the floor below mine. I listened, hard, but could hear nothing. Perhaps he was standing beneath me, his head raised to see if he could hear me too.

I tried to think, but everything was in motion, nothing fixed. And yet, in spite of it all, my heart began to steady itself. As my mother had once said, everything returns to the way it was: my nerves could not remain in such a heightened state. I felt myself beginning to calm as I stared at the door. I could not stay in my room for ever. I had to face what must be faced.

I stepped quietly through the silent house, my hand brushing the wall at my side. I went first to the drawing room, and after listening for a long moment at the door, went inside and approached the fireplace.

There was an empty space in the middle of the mantelpiece. To the right, a mourning card for my mother was propped against the wall; to the left was a replica of her wedding flowers, set in wax and protected by a glass dome. Of the bronze bull that had been placed between them, there was no sign.

Had my father just now removed it, knowing what I had seen – or had it never been replaced after what he did? I tried to remember the last time I had seen it and could not. I pictured him grasping my hair, dragging me to the top of the stairs. Raising his hand. I wondered if I would reach out in entreaty, beg for my life. I imagined the wooden risers breaking my limbs, shattering my spine, crushing my skull. I saw the way he would stand by my grave, accepting the sympathy of his acquaintances, history repeating itself.

I could almost hear the rueful tone of his voice. *And she the image of her mother at that age...*

I shook my head, thinking of the stifling rooms all about me, the little labyrinth in which I was obliged to live. I thought of the bull – the Minotaur, contained and yet so much more difficult to slay. What had my mother done with her pictures? They had achieved nothing but place me in danger. And yet would I wish to live here in ignorance, moving from one room to another and back again in this limited and airless circle, never knowing the truth?

I closed my eyes, trying to sense her, pleading with her to tell me what I should do – and her face rose before me. It was not contorted with fear or pain but sweetly smiling, and her lips moved, but there was no message there for me, nothing I had not heard before. I already knew the words that were on her lips.

It always goes back...

Suddenly, I understood what she was trying to tell me.

I hurried up the stairs, going first to my mother's room to gather the things I would need and then to my own, moving feverishly, throwing what I could into a portmanteau. I carried the bag into the hall before looking towards my father's study. I knew that he was in there. I sensed the life on the other side of it, the breath going in and out of his body. What thoughts must lie within that form? I could not fathom them.

After a moment, I pushed open the door. My father was seated at his desk, slumped in a posture of despair, his head in his hands. I saw, with little surprise, that the bull was within his reach.

But I was no longer afraid. I was no carven statue; no chains bound me to the wall. I walked towards him, past him, to the cupboard farthest from me, and found the thing I needed, my back towards him, and I turned, and still he did not raise his head.

The pistol, a remnant of his military service, was heavy in my hands; heavier than I had anticipated.

I went to his side. He must have heard the sound it made as I placed it on the desk, next to the bronze bull, but he made no sign. He did not speak and nor did I. There was nothing left to say.

I heard the report of the pistol, though, as I stepped from the front door, and shortly afterwards, Nella's shriek. I supposed I could have stayed to see the end – but what remained for me there? Only a house laden with unpleasant memories. I had with me everything of value my mother had owned – her jewellery, some bonds – her legacy to me. That was all I would need to begin my journey, not of existence, but of *life*.

I was fortunate to hail a hansom just outside the door and I stepped into it, placing my bag at my feet. I smiled as we drove away, listening to the rhythmic clatter of the horse's hooves against the granite setts. I had not troubled to bring the zoetrope with me. I would not need it any longer. And I rather liked the idea of someone going about the house to seek me there, passing from room to room and finding the device where it had always stood, on the old cabinet. I pictured them spinning the cylinder and bending to peer through the slit to see what I had placed within: a return to the beginning of it all, the first thing we had looked at together. They would not see me imprisoned within its walls, or my mother, or my father; they would see only the image of an endlessly galloping horse.

The Marvellous Talking Machine

It is across a distance of years that I remember the events of 1846, and yet it might have been yesterday that I first heard the voice that haunts my dreams. It is not the words that have troubled me so, ever since I was a boy; it is the way they were spoken – and the fact of their emerging from no human throat.

I was twelve when I first heard of the inventor Professor Joseph Faber. Now my hair is grey, though inwardly I feel much the same. I still remember my father's theatre, the magnificence of its halls; the sense of never knowing what wonders would pass before my eyes; the idea that perhaps, truly, they were not entirely of this world.

My father set me to work early, not because we were in need of funds, but because I begged him to release me from the tyranny of slate and desk. For what were schoolrooms to me, when life itself – and such life – passed daily before my eyes at the Egyptian Hall?

The edifice itself was a curiosity to behold. Part of the row of mansions lining Piccadilly, it was yet a thing apart; for its gargantuan figures, winged globes and lotus motifs would be better suited to an ancient tomb of Egypt than the heart of London. The mysteries continued within. Vast pillars suggested the great avenue at Karnak, while indecipherable hieroglyphics adorned every surface. Its ever-changing displays were equally entrancing, having included extraordinary statuary, dioramic views, historical artefacts – including Napoleon's coach – and indeed human entertainments; we had hosted a family of Laplanders offering sleigh rides, the Anatomic Vivante or Living Skeleton, and a mermaid – this last, alas, sadly pretend.

Indeed, it might be said that I was accustomed to wonders, and yet, when faced with something more remarkable still, I longed only to turn my face away. But I was not alone in that, for Joseph Faber's was one of our most poorly received attractions.

My first sight of the man was not promising. He was a hunched fellow, wearing a frock-coat with too few buttons, and those dulled with time. His beard was untrimmed, his shoes smeared with street-dirt and his features were unprepossessing; his eyes, which were dull likewise, looked askance when he was addressed, even by me, a mere child.

He gave his name softly and with a slight German accent. It was only when he directed the placement of his boxes and crates that his expression became sharp, even mercurial in his assiduousness. I showed him to the chamber wherein his display would appear and he glared about before closing its door in my face, presumably to prepare himself. Later, my father sent me to offer any assistance he may require. I knocked and a voice responded with some phrase that I had no doubt meant 'Go away'.

I did not go away, however, for I was young and curious; or perhaps it was stupidity that made me press my ear to the door and listen.

He was constructing something: that was certain. I decided I must ask my father what it was, for I had been much distracted by the imminent arrival of General Tom Thumb, a fellow celebrated for his diminutive stature and comic scenes, and had paid little attention when he told me of it. I knew only that it was some kind of machine, and so it seemed, for I detected the sound of wood being slotted into place and the clearer sound of metal striking metal. But it was Faber's mutterings that interested me the most.

It did not sound as if he were talking to himself. He would murmur in a low voice and then pause so that I could sense him listening before giving some reply. It sounded as if he were engaged in conversation with someone I could not quite hear.

Suddenly my ear stung as my father cuffed it. He told me to step sharp and see about the scenery flats in the main theatre, in tones so loud that Faber, shut up in his room, must surely have heard. And so I left him in there, alone yet not alone, speaking to whoever would listen; and to prepare for his performance that evening, whatever that may be.

~

I stared down at the handbill. THE MARVELLOUS TALKING MACHINE, it proclaimed. I had wasted no time, after dressing the stage for the hilarious capers of Tom Thumb, in obtaining a copy from the ticket-seller.

So here was the answer to the sounds I'd heard coming from Professor Faber's room. The bill informed me that not only could his machine speak, but that a full explanation would be given of the means by which the words and sentences were uttered. It said that visitors may examine every part of his Euphonia – that was what he named it – not only demonstrating a wonder of science, but providing a fund of amusement to young and old alike.

All at once, I understood. Examination notwithstanding, it was clear to me that Faber was a cheat; for of course he must have some accomplice who would be concealed within this 'wondrous' machine and speak on its behalf. It had been done before. Almost a hundred years ago, Kempelen's chess-playing Turk was heralded as the most magnificent automaton of its age, until it was discovered that its contests were won by a mere human hiding within its base. Thus it was made plain: it was a feat of wonder for a machine to mimic a man, but a matter of imposture and derision for a man to mimic a machine.

I could not confront Faber or reveal him as a fraud, however, for were we not his hosts, and party to all that passed? Yet I was determined to see for myself how the trick was done, and I confess I longed to lay eyes on whatever little creature may be concealed so cunningly. For, of course, it occurred to me that he or she may prove even tinier than Tom Thumb himself.

My disappointment may only be imagined when my father asked me to sort through a heap of mouldering costumes, to put some aside for repair, others for disassembling and yet others for the ragman. I knew I would never finish in time to take my seat for the start of Faber's demonstration, and it being held in a somewhat small chamber, I could not then disturb those who had paid their shilling by making my entrance.

Still, as the time came for it to end, I could not resist waiting in the passage to glimpse what I may when the doors opened. This time, I could more distinctly make out the sounds from within. People called out in turn, the audience I supposed, and something answered, though in tones the like of which I had never encountered. The voice was flat and dead and empty, and it made me shudder, and then the first notes of music sounded, and the awful voice began to sing. It was the National Anthem, but emotionless and dry, as if the life was missing, or perhaps the soul; as if the voice progressed from the very heart of a tomb. But of course this must be Faber's Talking Machine, his Euphonia, and I grasped the reason at once. For he could not wish it to sound human; if it did, all would guess at its true nature and his imposture would be discovered. It must perforce sound like something long dead – indeed, like something that had never lived. And yet I could not quite shake the chill as I pressed my eye to the keyhole.

But the door suddenly shook and swung open. I started back; a gentleman stood there, with commodious whiskers and a gloriously shining top hat. He gave me a disdainful look before leading the exodus from the room, and I made a hasty bow, gesturing towards the exit as if I'd come especially to point the way.

All the ladies and gentlemen filed past me, and as they went, I realised something odd about them. Usually, our patrons left smiling and laughing, exclaiming over what they had seen. But these did not smile; they did not laugh. They were entirely silent as they moved towards the cabs and carriages that awaited. There was no light in their faces; the only emotion emanating from them was dismay.

I looked away from them and saw Faber, his skin pallid, his eyes as lightless as the rest – and fixed upon mine.

I mouthed an apology, catching a glimpse of the contraption behind him: a wooden frame, through which I could see the back of the stage; an arrangement of keys and levers and bellows; and, affixed to its front, a human face. It was in the form of a woman – or rather, a girl – with bow lips and gleaming ringlets, but with a cold and empty expression. It unnerved me to look upon it, and I knew in that instant there was nowhere for anyone to hide, even if they were half the size of Tom Thumb.

Faber stepped towards me and I turned and closed the door between us. I did not leave, however, but leaned heavily against the wall. Thankfully, he did not follow; after a time I heard shuffling sounds and the scraping of wood against the floor.

Then I heard a soft call of 'Gute nacht'.

I froze, thinking he called out to me, then the light that crept from under the door was extinguished and I was left in near darkness. Faber was to sleep in the chamber, then, with his machine. Whatever his trick, it seemed I would not discover it that evening.

~

The next day, I asked my father what he knew of the strange inventor who remained ensconced within our chamber. In response, he pulled a face.

'His takings are underwhelming,' he said.

I opened my mouth to enquire further and found myself unsure what it was I sought. However, he went on regardless.

'He's a scientist, not a performer, and a mad one at that. This isn't his first talking machine, did you know? He burned the first one.'

'Why did he do that, Papa? Didn't it work?'

He looked as if he'd like to spit. 'Who knows? Drove himself maniacal with it, I reckon. It's clever – more than clever, some would say – but people don't like it all the same. There's some asked for their money back.'

'It really speaks, then, his machine?'

My father affirmed that it did, and I remained silent, musing on that. It seemed intolerably sad to waste such an effort, if the professor really had somehow made the thing work. But perhaps his first attempt had failed?

I did not realise that I had voiced my feelings until my father replied. 'Sad, you say? There's worse things, boy. Sleeps in the same room with it, he does. Insists he can't leave it by itself. It's not good for a man to become so obsessed – mark that. And—'

'Yes, Papa?'

He hesitated before he spoke and when he did it was with reluctance, as if it were something better left unsaid. 'It's just – I did hear tell he's given that machine his dead sister's face.'

I recoiled, thinking for an instant he meant it was made from flesh and blood; but of course it could not be so. I remembered the Euphonia's visage, her bow lips, her pretty ringlets – her lifeless eyes. And it came to me of a sudden that 'euphonious' meant pleasant, honeyed, bell-like; agreeable. How could Faber give his deathly sounding machine such a name – and such a face, one that was dear to him? But of course, he could not have meant it to sound as it did. Perhaps that was why he had been driven mad, why he burned his first machine; he must have realised the gulf between what he hoped to achieve and reality. And yet, if his machine could truly speak, he was responsible for a miracle – was he not?

~

That evening, I witnessed the miracle for myself.

I did not know if Faber saw me as I scuttled inside and took a seat at the back of the room. I did not see him, only his machine, its pale face and shining hair standing out from the shadows. The edges of the room were dimly lit, though the stage was bright with gaslights, hissing and sputtering and highlighting each strut and lever and key – making it abundantly clear to all that no one could be concealed within. Those lights would not be lowered, not for this performance. Everyone could see as much as they wished.

Faber stepped forward. In a halting voice, he begged the liberty of introducing us, one and all, to his Marvellous Talking Machine, his Euphonia. His voice softened when he spoke

- 39 -

its name, and he looked upon the immobile face with something like affection. I saw that he had hung a white dress beneath it for this performance; a dress that hung limp and empty almost to the floor, swinging slightly in some unseen draught. The hem, I noticed, was a little frayed, and I wondered where he had come by it. Had this, too, been his sister's?

Faber took his seat at the instrument as at a pianoforte, stretching his hands from his sleeves like a great proficient before placing them above a set of ivory keys.

A noise like a great intake of breath filled the room. It was the only sound; no one moved or spoke. Then the Euphonia opened her mouth. Slowly, so slowly, she said, with a slight German accent, 'Please excuse my slow pronunciation. Good evening, ladies and gentlemen... It is a lovely day... It is a rainy day.'

I realised I was leaning forwards in my seat. Despite the ordinariness of the words, I was repulsed; fascinated. Her lips moved like human lips. Her tongue lolled within her mouth like a human's. She breathed like a human, and yet no one could mistake her voice for a human voice.

I think my feelings were shared, for it was only when she ceased speaking that those around me began to move again as people do, shifting in their seats, rubbing their lips. No one applauded, however. No one cheered.

I looked at Faber, whose mouth was compressed into an unhappy line, his brows drawn down.

He invited the audience to provide words for his machine to copy. One soul, braver than the rest, bid her say, 'Buona sera.'

No doubt he intended it for some trick, but say the words she did, though slowly, sounding each syllable as if she were learning his language. Another called out a line from *The Taming of the Shrew*. She could pass no comment upon it, only copy his words. Another demanded something about the fineness of the summer and this she spoke too, all with the same languor, although sunshine and warmth seemed a long way from this accursed chamber.

Then Faber demonstrated how, with the turn of a screw, the Euphonia could whisper. This was even worse. In this way she gave out the words of a hymn, though such a horror of a hymn I'd never heard. Still, I could not take my eyes from her empty gaze, until I became sensible that someone else was watching; someone standing at the back of the stage.

It was a girl, almost concealed by the curtain. Her hair was shining, her dress white, her face pale. I did not look at her directly but even from the corner of my eye, I could see that her lips were moving. Was this Faber's accomplice after all? I turned my head to better focus on her, and saw that no one was there. It was only a fold in the curtain, nothing more, and I shook my head. I told myself I was unsettled by the dreadful voice and the dismal man operating it. Little wonder he had burned his first effort – would that he had burned the second!

Then everyone around me rose from their seats, and I realised it was time to inspect the machine. I did not wish to go closer, yet I followed, not wishing to remain alone either, and in the jostling of the crowd I found myself standing directly before the Euphonia's face.

Close to, it appeared more lifeless than ever, more like a doll, and I wondered that I could have imagined it to be made of flesh. Faber explained its workings: the replicated throat and vocal organs made of reeds, whistles, resonators, shutters and baffles, and then he showed how the bellows drove air through it all, and the Euphonia opened her lips and let out a long exhalation. It felt like breath on my cheek, but cold – cold as the grave.

I started away from it and, hidden amidst the bustle, slipped from the room. I had heard the Euphonia speak. I had no wish, now, to hear her sing.

I could not keep away, however, for after the crowds had dispersed, I returned to that little room. I did not know what drew me there, only that I had been unable to cast it from my mind. Perhaps it was pity for poor mad Professor Faber. I expected to find him lost in despair at the horror induced by the thing he loved, but no; even from the passage I could hear voices and the clanking of keys.

Quietly, I opened the door and slipped inside. He was seated once more at his infernal machine. He had not seen me enter, for his head was lowered as he played upon it. The Euphonia's mouth gaped and twisted. She was singing after all, but not *God Save the Queen* or any such thing. I had not heard its like before, but I guessed this must be some German nursery song, perhaps even a lullaby.

My gaze went to the place by the curtain where I had imagined seeing a young girl. With those sepulchral tones resounding all about me, I could almost believe I had truly glimpsed the spirit of his dead sister.

Faber suddenly let out a cry of despair and slumped across his machine, folding his arms before his face.

And yet – I can see it still – the Euphonia sang on. Her lips continued to move; her eyes still gazed blankly at me, holding me there until her song was done.

Slowly, Faber began to unwind his arms and lift his head. I did not wait to see his sorrow, or whatever message his expression might hold. I grasped for the door again, pulled it open and I fled.

~

That was many years ago. Faber left us soon afterwards, saying he had an opportunity with Barnum in America, and yet success was never his. I heard sometime later that he had destroyed his beloved Euphonia once more; and he too had then perished, by his own hand. It seemed plain to me, upon receiving the news, that they must always have risen or fallen together.

And could I believe that his was only a machine – that the glimpsed figure was an illusion conjured by my overwrought imagination? Sometimes, perhaps. But more often it seemed to me that he created not a Talking Machine, but a vessel; and that something immeasurably distant yet always close to him had come to reside within it.

I have thought upon it more than ever after my wife, Mary, passed away. Like Faber, we had no children. My father died long before; I was the last of my line. I was grown old and was alone, and lonely. Mary went before me into the dark, and I wondered: what would I not do to bring her back, to have my dear wife speak to me again?

The question would have signified nothing, of course, if it were not for the parcel addressed to me that arrived at the Egyptian Hall, years after Faber's death, but not long after my wife's.

The writing within was in a tongue strange to me, yet I saw its purpose at once. For there were plans and diagrams within: plans with levers and keys and shutters and baffles, and an empty space where a face should be.

Some unknown beneficiary of the professor must have sorted through his sad possessions at last – yet it seemed almost meant to be. It appeared that Faber had not been able to entirely destroy his life's work, but had decided to pass it on, to let some other man decide whether it should live or die. The only name he had bethought himself to write on the stained, torn envelope containing all his wisdom was mine.

And I began to dream of it, that awful, dry, dead voice whispering as I slept. Would it be worth the cost, I wondered, to have my wife speak, but in such a voice – dead – soulless? But perhaps, I told myself, it needn't be so. I pored over the plans with increasing avidity. Could not the arrangement of baffles be improved upon a little? And the whistles and resonators could surely be of finer make than had been available to Faber. If I followed the plans carefully, exactly, yet made my own little improvements here and there, surely the vessel would be perfect. I would hear her the way she was in life, her honeyed tones, her bell-like laughter...

I could only pray it would be so. It took many more months of hearing that voice, of wondering, but eventually I could resist its call no longer. I had the papers translated piecemeal, so that none but I would learn their whole secret. And I started to build, creating lungs, glottis, vocal cords, tongue, lips. I laboured long in closed rooms, my beard becoming unkempt, my clothes as stained as Faber's had been. It consumed me, this thing, and yet still I hoped.

Now it is nearing completion. With his footsteps carved into the earth before me, I have achieved what cost Faber many years of torment. Soon it will be time to take my place at the machine and see what emerges from its waiting lips.

~

The time has come to try my creation. I sit at its keys, regretting the arrangement that has Mary's face turned outward, so that I cannot see it. I wonder what expression might be revealed upon it? But it is of no matter. If my wife returns to me, I will know. I will feel her presence.

I place my hands so that they are just resting on the ivories, and fill her artificial lungs with air. She takes a breath. We are ready.

I touch my fingers to the keys, and in answer she begins to speak. I press and press and her vowels turn into words that become sentences, and still I cannot stop, though I want to; with my whole heart, I want to. But my fingers betray me. They keep pressing, performing their dance, and I do not know what drives them; perhaps it is horror. Perhaps it is only that I wish, so very badly, that it is not true...

The voice speaks with a German accent. It is unmistakeable, even in its hoarse whisper. And there is so little life in it that I can almost convince myself I am wrong, but as it speaks to me, I know: the voice is not a woman's, but a man's. It is Faber's voice I hear.

I sense a presence, though not hers, not the one I longed for so badly. I can picture the dishevelled, hunched figure standing at my back, watching me with narrowed eyes. I feel his sorrow, his yearning, his unfathomable despair, and still, I play. I make my machine whisper. I make it sing, but even then, the truth does not change.

I press my hands to the keys more firmly than ever. I am driven onward by something – madness, perhaps; yes, it is likely that. And yet there is fascination too, with the terrible miracle that is before me. Most of all, I realise it is fear. For what would happen if I ceased giving it these words – my words? The thing might not stop speaking. It might keep opening its lips – and what might I hear then?

I keep feeding it, and as I do, I feel my own humanity slipping from me. I do not mourn it as it goes. I think of Faber shutting himself in a room, setting fire to his machine, to himself. I can almost sense the flames that await me, that are waiting to consume us both.

Meet Me
at the
Frost Fair

It was a drab and dreary evening when Mr
Samuel Metcalf, a well-known inhabitant of the
corner seat at my club, began to expound upon
the glories of all the Christmases of his youth.
I had left wife and hearth to dine there that
evening and was sitting in a wing-back chair
close by the fire, half nodding as it hissed and
spat. It was December, and the sky beyond the
windows would already have been quite dark,
was it not for a pale yellow fog pressing itself
against the panes. It was damp also; occasionally
the pattering of a thin drizzle intervened,
lending an especially dismal aspect to the world
without.

Inside, all was comfort. The port wine was
rich and warming; the fire was high and merry,
with all its crackling; the furniture was of
decently gleaming mahogany and all was lent a
richness by the crimson paper lining the walls
and the deep, soft Turkey carpet. Hence I was a
little startled when Metcalf opened with, 'What

an evil night it is! Curse this dank misery. Do you remember what it was to be a boy, Radcliffe?'

My beard and whiskers had long since turned to grey; thus, his statement was less one of presumption than sincere mutual recollection, since his own pate was quite innocent of hair, his form given to stoutness and his visage to wrinkles. I merely inclined my head, certain there was more to follow, as indeed there was.

'Grey!' he said next. 'Grey as cobwebs, and everything chill and damp. Some proper snow is what we need, Radcliffe! What happened to the winters of old? Everything dressed in white, with ice gleaming from the rooftops, the air crisp and clean, untainted by all these smuts and cinders. Throwing snowballs and skating on the Serpentine – ah, that was it! These miasmas and vapours are nothing to it. The rule of Jack Frost was far preferable – I say, don't you agree?'

I could not suppress a chill, though I inhaled deeply of my pipe, exuding my own blue-grey vapour. 'Thus men ever romanticise their youth.'

'Not you, I suppose? You prefer this foul fog? Why, one can hardly see one's hand before one's face! They say another man died yester-evening, for losing his way and falling into the river.' He wrinkled his nose in disgust, and well he may; for the stench of the befouled Father Thames had reached even here, and would be in our nostrils, I knew, the moment we stepped from the door.

I sighed, suddenly remembering the mad slip and dash of blades upon the ice, its surface scarred by the delighted passing of so many boys and girls, the pinched faces, the red noses, the grins... I pushed the memory from me. 'On the surface, the past may have been better,' I said, 'but it could be more perilous also. And we have so many comforts now. The iron rail is bringing down the cost of coal' – I gestured towards the fire – 'and progress must surely increase a thousand-fold, with our new queen on the throne, and—'

'Nonsense!' he cried. I did not protest, for such was ever Metcalf's way. He was a man of busyness, and had never had the time, as he once explained to me, for any particular excess of manners. 'It's all going to ruin, Radcliffe – admit it! Why, my good coat was only this morning waylaid by such a cloud of coal-smuts the finest laundress in London couldn't save it. No! Look at that window, now. What a little of Jack Frost's breath could not do to cheer it, with a pattern of icy leaves? The sooner he should return, the merrier it shall be for all.'

'All?' I murmured the word, for I was thinking of something else. It had been the second time he'd mentioned the name of Jack Frost, and I shifted uncomfortably in my seat.

'Then pray, tell me what of today is better,' he said, 'since I see I cannot persuade you.'

I felt a chill, despite the proximity of the flame. 'Very well,' I replied, still in the same drowsy murmur, and I took a sip of port wine and made up my mind. 'I *shall* tell you, though not of what you are thinking. I shall tell you why it would perhaps be better for the name of Frost never to be spoken within these walls again, or any other. For cold is as cold does, and a cold heart is something to be feared as well as—'

'What bosh you do speak this evening, sir!' he said, although his tone spoke of amusement. 'Still, I shall listen, if you will only allow me to fill my glass.'

I did so, and the sight of the rich liquid, lent fiery heart by the firelight, heartened me. I *would* tell my tale, I decided, though until that moment I'd been uncertain of doing so. It was not really my story to tell, on one count; on another, I knew that even thinking upon it would make me feel colder still. Yet Metcalf settled back, his face lit with a ruddy glow, his eyes half hidden by the shadows cast by his wing-backed seat. Such is how tales *should* be told, I thought, by the warming fire; and so I began.

'My tale opens years ago, in 1788. A bitter frost began on the twenty-fifth of November, and continued some seven weeks. Its severity was such that even our great river was turned to iron in its grip. Ah, you don't have to impress upon me what a wonder that must have been, Metcalf; I saw it for myself. At first, a few intrepid souls ventured forth, half afraid, half laughing; and then others bolstered their resolve and followed. It was found that men could walk right across the river and need no longer pay to use the bridges. Indeed, it was possible to walk from Fulham to Putney that year, so frozen over was the water. It was no mere convenience, but a novelty; and it gave the closing of that year and the opening of the next quite a festival air. As you stated, all was overspread with pure white; and yet it was not long to be so, for soon the river was bedecked with all colours, as it was given over to entertainments of every variety.'

'A frost fair? Alas, I did not see it.'

'Indeed, Metcalf! A frost fair was held that year, as in many before it. Gradually, everything designed for amusement or diversion crept onto the frozen river. There were fairground booths of all descriptions, puppet shows, turnabouts for the children, and every hue of hawker and peddler; even wild beasts were exhibited there, shivering though they must have been. Sheep and pigs were roasted and eaten upon the ice. A bear was baited, and drew all the multitudes who desired to witness such a thing. And walking among the rest was one Mister John Langton – known as Jack – a young fellow whose family was acquainted with my own. I was twenty-five, he a little younger; and he was yet unmarried, though he did not walk there alone. For although he stepped onto the Thames an eligible bachelor, when he stepped from it his heart was lost.'

Metcalf snorted. 'Do you tell me a story of the heart, Radcliffe? I had thought you above such frippery.'

I gave a slight bow. 'All in good time, for I am forgetting our theme; that of the superiority, or otherwise, of the past. It was a time of merriment, as I have said, though I have neglected my part, which is to show that it was also a time of great want. For although the Thames became a stage for all the gaudy shows the city could boast, its banks were full of abject misery. The bustling trade of the river was brought to a halt. Watermen and fishermen had no means of earning their bread, and corn and coal vessels alike were stilled. Prices rose and the nights were cold, and fuel of any kind was hard to come by. All this resulted in the most desperate need amongst the poor, and although subscriptions were raised, they couldn't hope to fill the hungry maw of winter.

'Still, what of that? For the Thames was there in all its gleaming whiteness to lend a little cheer to those who most required it. Not a countenance was there to be seen upon its broad back that wasn't filled with delight, and so our young fellow set out, a smile on his lips and coins in his pocket, to see what the season held for him.'

'A female, I suppose?'

'A female,' I agreed. 'And such a female! The young lady was with her parents, as was proper, though fortunately for the fellow he was known to her father; and so as he stood watching the printing presses which had been hauled onto the ice, staining white paper with commemorations of the occasion, he found himself hailed and introduced to the gentler members of the family. In later years, he expressed to me how strange it was that he could bring himself to speak coherently. He told me of her sweet lip and soft smiles and her dimples and shining eyes, and yet I still do not know if she were fair or dark. I only know, from his account, that she was a vision; and that he was the most fortunate man on earth to be the object of her attention as they wandered about. For he was the unworthy recipient to whom she gave her arm, and he rejoiced at the uncertainty of their steps upon the smooth surface, that she clung to him the more tightly.

'Adela was her name, though I knew from the way he spoke of her afterward, that he was already longing for her to change it to Mrs Langton; and perhaps that was how he envisaged her, as a bride, all aglow in a gown the colour of ice.

'But before all that there were booths to peruse, and jugglers to watch, and tumblers to behold; a coach trotting along the middle of the river to marvel at; and boys whirling about them on their skates to provide the cause of some pretty alarm. All was charming, save for a single incident which promised to spoil the beauty of the whole.

'It occurred after Jack had reluctantly taken his leave of the lady and began to make his return to the steadfast shore. A poor woman stood at the side of the river, her feet mired in the muddy banking, a ragged shawl clutched about her shoulders. Her nose ran with the cold and her face was pinched; she was an unfortunate creature, and made a pitiful, if not distasteful sight, to those grown fond of revelry. They turned aside as well as they could to avoid her, though in doing so there arose some difficulty. For the mud was so melted and stirred by the passing of numerous feet that a plank had been placed to ease their egress; and the woman stood by it, ankle-deep in filth, so that she could hold out her palm towards those who walked across.

'At once, our soft-hearted fellow put his hand to his pocket; but he discovered that the purchases he had made on behalf of the lady had left him with only a penny, which he required to pay his way across the plank. Thus he turned his eyes from the woman, who, seeing the indifference of one too many of her fellow-beings, gave way to despair. She turned from him, and in so doing fell to her knees, while he stepped onto the dry path.

'She regained her feet with some difficulty; then she rushed towards him and spat on his boot. The fellows taking payment for the use of their plank chased her off at once, but the impression she had left upon Jack's mind was not so easily effaced. For he couldn't cast off the notion that her anger had left some stain, not upon his attire, but his soul; and that some dreadful misfortune might follow what had surely amounted to a curse.'

'She should have been flogged.'

'Ah – is it possible to flog the rudeness from poverty? It is easier, perhaps, and more charitable, to give a little bread to those who need it. And yet I suspect it is because he had truly wished to do so that it weighed so heavily upon him. Still, he was comforted; for Miss Adela had not witnessed the event and soon after, the lady of his heart consented to be his wife. They walked upon the ice once more before it melted away. They went there together, promised to each other, united in sincere love and adoration, and almost over-brimming with joy.'

Metcalf made a sort of harrumph at this, shifting in his seat, and I recollected that his was not the contempt of the loveless but of one who had lost; his wife had died some years previously. More than anyone, he could be said to know the ending of all such stories, and I hesitated before I went on.

'They were married in the spring,' I said, 'and enjoyed perfect domestic felicity. The frosts had passed, and all was life. Still, within a very short time, his wife began to sicken. By the summer she had taken to her bed, and before the season was out he was called to her room, where the doctor feared for her life.

'Jack's distress may be imagined. He chafed her hands; he implored God and all his angels to save her; he shed bitter tears. Still her breath faltered in her lovely throat and at last she beckoned him closer.

'He was silenced, he later told me, by the sight of her. Her cheeks were pale and shrunken, yet her eyes were undiminished, still shining as brightly as her love. And she opened her sweet lips and whispered to him, before she died: "Meet me at the frost fair."'

I fell silent, suddenly conscious of the quietness of the room. The thought of death seemed to have lent substance to the air; then Metcalf sighed and the spell was broken.

'She went to her last eternal rest,' I said, 'and Jack was plunged into despair. Yet not quite despair, for her final words remained, and he clung to them, and he waited for winter, the season that had brought him his love. I saw him myself, sitting by the Thames, staring into the water and longing for the cold; for the beginnings of ice to form at its edges like bridal lace. And yet it did not come. There was to be no frost fair all that winter, and as one year gave way to the next he began to fade; even to wither. His coat hung loose upon his shoulders. His complexion turned pale with watching, and when he spoke his words came with difficulty, as if his mind, too, had begun to freeze.'

Metcalf tutted. 'But it was the same the year after that, was it not? And the next. The days of decent winters were passed, as I have said.'

'They had,' I allowed. 'For over twenty years, Jack Langton waited in vain. Then, in 1814, his hour finally arrived. It had been a long time by then since I'd seen him, and I was shocked at the changes time had wrought. But I am running ahead.

'I saw the beginnings of the fair myself. At the end of January, enormous masses of ice floating down from the upper part of the river were trapped by the narrow arches of London Bridge. I walked there that evening to partake of the singular sight, and returned two days afterwards to find that severe frosts had turned the river into one solid surface all the way down to Three Crane Stairs. I was not the first to discover it, however. Half of London was out on the ice, and their good cheer at such a novelty seemed to form a glowing cloud above it all. I confess, I never thought of Jack, and had not for several years. I simply stepped onto the gleaming surface and tried to peer through it to the black depths beneath. It was fearful and wonderful and I had to rein in my delight as I walked along, seeing the booths and stalls all got up in streamers and ribbons, surrounded by revellers giddy on gin or rum. It was as if Christmas, so soon lost, had returned to us again.

'I began to make my way along the grand mall that led between London Bridge and Blackfriars. They had named it "The City Road," and what a road it was! It was lined with stallholders selling toys labelled "bought on the Thames"; couples danced to fiddler's wild tunes outside the drinking tents; the reckless played rouge-et-noir or te-totem for coin; others bowled at skittles or set their children on the swings. Yet not all was merriment. As I walked I saw, at first in glimpses and then plainly, that one fellow was not looking at the stalls; he wasn't even moving along the road. Fair-goers were edging around him, the ladies holding their skirts clear as if his touch might be tainted. I went a little closer and realised he was sitting upon the ice. He was clad in black and the colour of mourning almost seemed spill from him along with a miasma of bitterness and desolation.

'I thought for a moment of helping him – then my attention was drawn away, for downriver, a great grey beast was being led onto the ice. Cries rang out of "Elephaunt, elephaunt!" I had never seen such a thing before and hurried to join the crowds being drawn in its wake like a tide.

'By the time I returned, the sun was setting and the moon had risen, lending the ice a lambent glow as bewitching as it was peculiar. The sight of the gleaming expanse, the great dome of Saint Paul's and all the sprawling life of London beyond, was one I shall never forget. The only blot upon the day was my memory of the man sitting upon the ice, and I was relieved, as I walked once again along The City Road, that he was no longer there.

'Then, to my left, I heard a shriek. I turned to see a lady dressed in fine watered silk throwing up her hands; a group of apprentices jeering; serving girls pointing and tittering. And I saw what had so startled them.

'That same dark figure was at their centre, and he was dancing. He was dancing as if he were in a ballroom, his back straight and his neck held high. He advanced and retired; he bowed to some unseen partner; and then he reached out and clasped nothing but the air. There was no music yet he danced on, his eyes half-closed, his expression beatific. It was only then that I realised it was none other than my old acquaintance, John Langton. But how changed! His cheeks were hollow, his eyes sunken in their sockets. His nose seemed beak-like in his thin visage, his chin pointed; his wax-like pallor was almost that of a cadaver. And he was so wasted that he put me in mind of a skeleton – a skeleton prancing on the ice. He had not quite passed into death, however, for as he danced, tears slipped from his cheeks.

'He appeared so lost, and yet so sad and happy all at once, that although I stepped forward to hail him – to *stop* him – again, I failed to offer him any assistance. Indeed, I found myself frozen. Moonlight limned his features, his flying hair, the tears that lay upon his cheek. And I almost thought I saw someone held in his arms after all. I caught the merest suggestion of a form, yet even in that glimpse I knew it was a lady of uncommon loveliness; and she was dressed in shining ice.

'For the first time that day, I felt cold to my bones. I found myself, instead of helping the man, backing away from him, and then I turned and left, trying to calm my beating heart, to drown the spectres that haunted my thoughts in all the ordinary sights of the fair.

'I did not stop until I stood before one of the printing presses, which that year was producing the frontispiece for a book – *Frostiana: or a History of the River Thames in a Frozen State*. The word echoed through my mind like a whisper – *Frostiana* – but it wasn't the river I was thinking of. It was that half-glimpsed maid, clasped in the arms of her love.

'*"Meet me at the frost fair,"* she had once said to him, and I do believe she had found him at last.'

'He was a madman,' Metcalf said, though his voice was soft. 'And you were somewhat credulous, if I may say so, good fellow.'

'Perhaps,' I replied. 'In any event, a day or so later the wind turned to the south, and soon after that the rain began to fall. The ice plain thinned; black water could be heard welling from beneath, and soon loud cracks resounded from the ice, followed by the most unearthly moans.

'The frost fair was at an end. Those who lingered soon saw their peril. Two young men ventured out onto a piece of ice which broke from the rest and carried them away; it tilted and they sank into the river and were seen no more. I feared for Jack, my old acquaintance, for if any should overstay upon the fragile surface it was he; but I didn't see him again until days afterwards. He had resumed his vigil at the water's edge, sitting in the cold drizzle and staring out once more at the river.'

'The fair lasted only four days, did it not?'

'It did.'

'So what did the fellow do? He sounded half crazed already.'

'Yet he would not be deterred from his purpose. And I do not think, really, that he was mad. It was more that his heart had grown colder than any heart was meant to be.

'Each winter that followed found him by the river. Each flake of snow brought hope; sunshine brought misery. I hadn't thought it possible that he could become gaunter still, and yet he did.

'I brought myself to approach him only once, thinking to turn him from his vigil. I sat at his side, and it was an odd thing, Metcalf, but I could still feel the bitterness that rose from him. It wasn't especially cold, not that day, but the chill crept into me all the same, curling itself about my bones. It robbed me of my voice and I didn't speak to him after all, nor shiver – not until he turned to me and I saw his eyes.'

'What was wrong with them?'

I shuddered despite the heat of the fire, which gave a sudden sharp crack, as if to remonstrate against my telling of such things, of making entertainment from another man's tale. 'They were cold,' I said simply, and could not elaborate. I couldn't explain my impression of all the frozen lakes of Hell reflected within them; the fact that I knew, despite Jack's presence in front of me, that he was already there.

'He did not speak?' Even Metcalf looked discomfited.

'He did,' I said, and swallowed. I could still hear Langton's voice, dry and harsh as any arid solitude of the poles. 'I still remember the words.

He said, "I believed the woman's curse had fallen to Adela, but it had not; it had not. It was ever and always my own." And with that he turned and resumed watching the river, which despite the coldness of his glare, steadfastly refused to freeze.'

'I think I see the end of your story,' said Metcalf, 'though I must say, dear fellow, I do not believe you have carried your point. A good winter would have been a blessing, would it not? He could have seen her then, or thought he did. It might have eased his heart.'

I bowed. 'Perhaps you are right, after all. And yet I only meant to show that constantly longing for what is past – for what we may not have again – is to waste everything that we are.' My tone was wistful, for as I spoke, I thought I heard the distant echo of the sound of my own youth: the scrape and hiss of skates on ice; the excited shouts; the laughter.

I sighed. 'But you say, Metcalf, you see the end of the tale. It is, I am certain, quite as you imagine. Not long before the ascension of our good queen, old London Bridge was torn down. Its replacement had wider arches that could never trap the ice floating upon the river, as the older bridge had. Not only that, but the climate has grown milder, as you so forcibly remarked upon. The ice will not creep from the edges of the Thames again. The days of the frost fairs are done.'

'So what became of your friend?'

They pulled him, dead, from the water, Metcalf, even as the new bridge took form. He had watched until he reached almost his seventieth year, until he knew all hope to be entirely lost.'

'Ah. A great pity.'

'It was,' I replied, 'or it should have been, if that had been the end of the matter, but it was not. He was still sitting there, you see. An acquaintance of mine swore that he'd spotted Jack by the river, in his accustomed place, staring into the water.'

'A mistake.'

'I thought so. But the next day brought further news. A recently married couple, full of affection for one another, were walking by the riverbank. They stopped to observe the progress of the lighters against the tide. They were seated there for some minutes and then the lady turned to her husband and shrieked.'

Metcalf frowned.

'The man was dead. His eyes were open but they were blank and staring and a film had begun to creep across their surface, like ice. His skin had paled also, and when she reached out to touch him – he was frozen, Metcalf. Entirely frozen.'

'Are you saying—'

'I think Jack had taken him. He had made his heart turn cold – with his touch, perhaps – yes, I think that is possibly all it took.'

Metcalf let out a splutter that was not really laughter. 'Really, my dear fellow, anyone may freeze by the Thames. It carries chill air right from the sea estuary.'

I half smiled. 'Yet it was not so cold that the lady felt any discomfort,' I said. 'And you see, he was not the last. Each winter, there are others. I have come to watch for it. And I believe that John Langton – Jack – has become the thing of which you spoke so lightly. He has become Jack-in-the-frost; and it is by frost that he stops the breath. It is always a man he takes, always someone with much to lose, and a sweet wife left to mourn him.'

'Your tale is becoming a little outlandish, is it not?'

'Possibly. Probably. But I have seen it myself, with my own eyes. I have seen men frozen so solid one could knock upon their flesh, even when the weather has been mild. I can no longer deny the truth of it. And I cannot help but wonder what the unfortunates were thinking, as they looked out at the river. Were they too remembering the winters of their youth, the days when the world all turned to whiteness?'

'Now you are speculating.' Metcalf patted his hands against his knees and stood. 'But I have lingered too long by this fire, dear fellow. At least there shall be no danger of my freezing. At least until I step into that damnable fog!'

I glanced at the window. For a moment it did not appear foggy any longer; it was only dark. I suppressed a shudder as Metcalf took his leave. The fire was guttering and few remained at their cigars; it was almost time to depart. I went to the window, wondering if Mary was watching for me as I now watched Metcalf appear on the street below. The fog remained after all, yet his step was casual, swinging his cane. Then he paused, taking a coin from his pocket and pressing it into the hand of the pitiful urchin who earned his bread as a crossing-sweeper on the corner. Metcalf didn't cross the road, however. He continued into the night, wrapping his great-coat a little more firmly about his neck as he was lost to view.

I leaned in closer until my breath clouded the glass. And then my eyes widened, for it did not dissipate but continued to spread, misty paleness making its way across the pane, melting in some places and thickening in others until it had created the most lovely pattern of leaves and ferns.

I started away then approached again, putting my fingers to the glass. It was ice, despite the warmth that still emanated from the fire. It did not melt at my touch.

I turned about the room, looking at the next window and the next as ice crept across them – covering every one in beautiful ferns of frost. I let out a long breath and it emerged in a cloud, hanging in the air in front of me. My heart faltered; I caught hold of the back of a chair and swayed. My thoughts raced. Perhaps I could stay here tonight. I could sleep in a chair, remain safe by the fire. And yet I knew that I would not, because Mary was waiting for me: Mary, my own dear, sweet wife.

I took a steadying breath. She would laugh at my consternation. I couldn't give way to phantasms and wild ideas; I must go home. And it was not here, after all, that was the haunt of Jack Frost; that was the river, and I resolved to go nowhere near it on my homeward journey. Still, the thought remained: what if I had summoned him here with my tale – with my dreams of winters past?

I closed my eyes, reminding myself that I was a respectable fellow. Metcalf's words rang in my ears: *credulous. Outlandish.* Metcalf, who had no wife; who had no one to mourn him when he left this earth. But he had surely been right.

And so I went down the stairs, barely hearing my own footsteps. Instead, a new sound played about my ears, or rather the memory of one, growing louder as I approached the door; closer and more real. It was the rush of skates upon ice. I heard a chill wind playing in the trees, the joyful cries of children playing in the snow.

I reached the door, hesitating before I opened it. When I did, I half expected to see snowflakes billowing in the air, but of course there were none; nevertheless, I looked out upon a wonderland. The lamps had been lit and the fog was illumined with an interior glow, turning everything pale and indistinct. There was nothing and no one to be seen, only the emptiness of a shining world. For a moment I thought I heard crackling, as if someone were walking towards me across a thin layer of ice; then all was silence.

Meet me at the frost fair, I thought, and stepped into the whiteness that awaited me there; that had been waiting for a very long time.

The Ballad Box

The story goes that the sundial which once stood at the heart of Seven Dials had only six faces, casting its blessings upon every street meeting there except one. Before I came here, I imagined I would be able to spot which street that was – the one where I was bound – but now I looked upon these miserable environs, I could only be surprised that the whole vile rookery had not been torn down long ago.

From my vantage point at the centre of the crossroads, I could make out every form of degradation known to sad humanity. Every street was headed by a public house, each with its complement of customers despite the hour, drunk to a man. Outside them, each iron post had its own downtrodden dame leaning against it, watching in fear that her husband would spend his week's pay on ale before the rent man came. Behind the public houses were rows of homes which had no doubt been subdivided and divided again. Dubious characters haunted doorways. Gaudy ladies, unfortunate in situation and profession, showed passers-by their ankles, vying with one another in bawdy shouts.

Theirs was not the only sound. Raucous laughter spilled from gin-shops tucked away down alleyways. A man tormented a tin whistle at the far side of the square, its shrieking matched by that of ragged children bowling hoops across the cobbles. Rougher cries emanating from behind one of the public houses spoke of a brawl. And through it all fluted a sweeter, higher sound: birdsong, emerging from a stall selling such creatures, committed to cages and complaining plaintively of their plight.

There was no one of whom I felt able to enquire which was Little St. Andrew's Street, and so I picked my way between the loiterers and ne'er do wells, one hand covering the pocket wherein was concealed my watch, until I made out its name on a dirty sign. I turned down the road without hesitation, for I deserved no better; and when a man sees his fate set out before him he had better start towards it at once.

As I went, I heard the muted sound of a voice raised in song:

The rope it was ready, John Hobbs, John Hobbs.
Come, give me the rope, says Hobbs;
I won't stand to wrangle,
Myself I will strangle,
And hang dingle dangle,

John Hobbs, John Hobbs;
He hung dingle dangle, John Hobbs.

The verse was followed by a peal of delighted laughter, and I knew that I had found the place. This time there was no painted sign, but I spied a scrap of paper nailed to the door, alongside a tarnished knocker. Upon it was written:

Algernon Peberdy
Balladeer Nonpareil

The description was a trifle florid, and as yet unearned; Peberdy had only lately entered the trade of printing broadsheets, and was yet to make a name besides the likes of Pitts, Birt or 'catchpenny' Catnach. But I was scarcely in a position to protest.

I gave a rap on the knocker, and was torn between awaiting a response and wiping my fingers on my greatcoat when a stout woman bustled by me without a by-your-leave, and pushed open the door. I glimpsed a small, bare room within, laid with dusty floorboards, and the door was closing again upon it when I regained my equanimity and followed her inside.

A stern, narrow-faced woman, her eyes set too close together, was seated behind a counter. The lady who had pushed past me – I use the term advisedly, since lady she most certainly was not – went up to her, trailing an unwashed odour, and set down a coin with a sharp *click*.

The woman behind the counter retrieved a bundle of closely-printed papers and handed them over. Her customer took them and left, once more pushing past me without a look. A ballad seller, then, off to hawk her wares.

I followed her example and approached the counter, but its occupant did not at first see me; she was busy staring with some distaste at the filthy sixpence placed there. After a moment, she used a piece of paper to whisk it into some unseen receptacle where, judging by the *chink*, it joined a number of others.

I informed her that I had come by appointment to see Mr Peberdy.

Could people here sing, but never speak? She indicated with her eyebrows an open door at the back of the room, where I could just see the worn, bare risers of a staircase. I did not bid her adieu; I merely went towards them.

~

Mr Peberdy was a stolid man in a richly patterned, shining silk waistcoat, into the tiny pockets of which he liked to thrust his thumbs, stalking about the room in a manner which reminded me of a goose. His rubicund face was adorned with the vastest Piccadilly weepers I had ever seen, the wiry grey whiskers making him appear older, I fancied, than he really was.

'So,' he said, halting his stride by an open window, from whence emanated the constant rattle of a printing press from somewhere below, along with a very peculiar smell. 'You were at Fleet Street.'

I agreed that I had been.

'What brings you here to the Dials?'

'Ambition, sir.' It was a lie of course, and he knew it as well as I did, but he made no effort to prevent me going on. 'I hear that a man may make his reputation in this place. That, and – duty, sir. I feel it is of the highest calling, to deter mankind from following the sinful path of the most wretched of his fellows.'

His eyes bulged and he hid a cough behind his hand. Was it mirth he concealed, or disdain? It was of no matter. All he managed was, 'Indeed?'

'Oh yes, sir. Yours is a noble calling, and I believe I have some natural talent at it.' I reached for my pocket, steeling myself to recite the verses I had rapidly penned the previous evening, but he waved them away.

'All I need to know is, can you rhyme and can you count?'

'I can.'

'Then go to the room next door. They'll set you right. Half a crown a sheet. And none of that writing for Peter one day and Paul the next – your pen is mine, unnerstand? And be timely. All I ask. Rhyming and counting and *alacrity*, you hear?'

I did hear. I thanked the gentleman and made my exit, already trying to ignore the wild laughter spilling from the adjacent chamber.

There I found waiting for me two gentlemen in shirtsleeves, one sitting at a large and rather untidy desk, the other leaning against a windowsill, where was set an old wooden box. Both had short black beards and eyes that shone with amusement. They looked me up and down as I told them my name was Benjamin Coyle, and straightened their expressions enough to nod.

'I'm Joskins. He's Briggs,' one said, and I tried to mark which was which so that I could tell them apart, though I doubted my ability to do so.

'You can do the Flitch Murder,' said Briggs. 'Sentencing tomorrer. You'll need to do the last words and confession. 'Andle that, can you?'

I nodded. 'How do I find out what he says? Is there some informant in the prison to whom I should apply?'

They looked startled and spluttered with laughter once more. Briggs – or Joskins – asked, 'Where did 'e find you then, eh?'

'Fleet Street.'

'Oh, aye – we 'eard that bit. Lot o' claptrap about a *noble profession*, an' all.'

More laughter.

I straightened. 'The informant?'

I waited and they looked at me and I read the message in their eyes. I had not suspected such a thing, though of course I should have. My heart sank as I said, 'It is invention – all of it?'

'Now you're gerrin' it, lad.'

Joskins – or Briggs – hopped down from the window and took up a pen. 'Now, do you think the Strangler of Clapham's last words would be to 'is wife or 'is mistress?' He winked.

I sighed and went to the window, through which drifted the same peculiar odour I had noticed before. Through it I saw a small enclosed yard, where a brazier bubbled and smoked with foul liquid.

'Vinegar and potash,' a voice said at my side. 'Has to be done, if you wants to be paid.'

'I beg your pardon?'

'They boil the takings in it, don't they. They brings enough coin in, but none'll take it from 'em again. They reckon any coin got up from the Dials will be diseased.' He drew out the word: *Dis-eased*. 'So they boil every ha'penny, till they can pass it on. Till it's clean.'

I sniffed. 'A dreadful odour. However do you stand it?'

'You'll get used to it, new lad. It don't reek when you're mired right in it!'

He laughed once more. Were they always laughing? I supposed they were. I tried to imagine laughing with them, being one of them, and couldn't. I looked down once more at the boiling pot and thought of the coins twisting and turning in the searing substance, having their history stripped away; becoming clean again.

~

The next day found me sitting at a corner of that same untidy desk, pen in hand, trying to think of a word that rhymed with *bludgeon*. Joskins – or it might have been Briggs – was sitting on the sill, his hand tapping on the box, whistling the same interminable tune I'd heard sung when I first arrived.

I had been to the Old Bailey that morning and heard sentence pronounced on Jem Flitch, who had beaten in his wife's head with a cudgel. He was to hang, and I had to finish my account by noon, but my head was clouded; I kept seeing his face, shining with tears – for his wife or himself, I did not know.

I pushed the sheet away from me and sighed. 'If I may ask a question?' I said. 'I can understand Mr Peberdy wishing to know if I could rhyme – it is rather a requisite of a ballad writer – but why did he ask if I can count?' I had been wondering if that was some promise of future earnings, but I had been the subject of humour enough already, and felt it better not to mention it.

'Eight – six – eight,' Joskins said. 'The number of syllables to a line, see?'

'But the song you were whistling before – John Hobbs – followed no such pattern.'

'Ah, John Hobbs, John Hobbs, he hung dingle dangle... That ain't one of ours, lad. And John Hobbs ain't no murderer. He's a man what tried to sell 'is wife, though when he couldn't get rid o' her he tried to hang 'isself anyway.'

He chortled, but I did not. What I saw, suddenly and perfectly clearly, was the look upon my editor's face when he told me to get out of Fleet Street. He hadn't known anything for certain, but he had suspected, and that had been enough. I shook the image away before looking down at my verse, counting the beats on each line, and found I had fallen into it naturally. Still: *bludgeoned...*

'Did you and – our other colleague write all the ballads here? Are you ever late?' I tried to sound casual.

'Aye, we wrote 'em.' Joskins sounded suddenly cautious. 'All except one, o' course.' He patted the box that was placed on the windowsill. 'Thought we'd get to that.'

I frowned, not knowing what he meant. I hadn't paid the box much attention, but I did now, and I saw that it was older than I had thought; much older. The wood was desiccated and greyed, a little cracked about the ancient and rusty lock. For a moment I thought I detected a scent, something like pepper and cinnamon, though that surely wasn't possible under the constant odour of vinegar.

'This here's the black ballad,' Joskins went on. 'This was penned by Jack Ketch 'isself. You'll have heard of it.'

I relieved him of that assumption.

'The *hexecutioner.*' He added an aitch, as if that could increase the notoriety of the man, but of course, he needed do no such thing. Everyone had heard of Jack Ketch: King Charles II's henchman, a man so acquainted with evil some said it was the name of the Devil himself.

'It was broadsheets made Ketch famous,' he went on. 'That, and the way he beheaded Lord Russell.' He slammed a hand into his palm, making a vile squelching sound with his tongue against his teeth. 'Meant to take his head off with one blow, that was the game, but he just kept on and on, never quite finishing it, chopping and chopping till even the crowd were sick o' the blood. Imagine it: the screaming. Some said it was accidental, but the thing is, they said Russell had insulted Ketch just afore 'e stepped up to the block. You know what, new lad? Never insult the man with the haxe!'

He laughed and this time I forced myself to laugh with him.

'They say Ketch went away gloating, and he wrote a ballad 'isself, only none would say what's in it. No one can read it, see, without seein' his own black heart reflected there. Then their soul belongs to him – to Jack Ketch – the hexecutioner. Or the Devil, acourse.'

'Have you read it?'

He opened his eyes wide. 'Not me! I'm not brave enough for that. Course, the key's in that drawer, if you fancy a look.' He gave an unreadable smile. 'Course, you'll none o' that, will you? Not wiv all your fine *morals*, an' that.'

Shortly after that he left and closed the door behind him, leaving me alone with the empty room and the stench of boiling vinegar and the unfinished work and the old, old box, which may or may not contain a ballad written by the Devil himself. I stared at it and then glanced at the clock, which at that moment appeared more pressing. I would not rise to what was surely a jape at my expense; I had work to do, and would not have Mr Peberdy accuse me of being lacking in rhyme, number, or indeed alacrity.

~

I managed my task – barely – and Mr Peberdy sniffed over it and sent it down to be set, to keep the presses in their endless rattle. I had not seen them for myself, and could almost imagine the lower floors to house some chain-rattling captive dragon, its maw constantly open, gnashing its teeth for more of the lurid fare on which it fed.

Without pause, Peberdy gave me my next assignment. A young woman had been murdered, he told me. Ordinarily, she would not warrant a song – a handbill of the particulars would suffice – but for her respectability, the fine part of the City she hailed from, and indeed the dreadful state in which she was discovered: her clothing disordered, her innards laid open to the air.

'Make 'em weep,' he instructed, 'and they're sold. Might even 'elp bring the cove what done it to justice, yes? That'd suit you. Might be doin' him a favour, an' all – make him famous enough for a Staffordshire figurine, yes?' He grinned broadly enough to show his back teeth.

'An' don't screeve. You don't work for the papers now, lad. Though if you do it well enough, *they'll* happen pinch some details from *you*.'

A little later I stared out of the open window at the boiling coins below, wondering what the young lady's thoughts must have been. Had she ever been in love? Was the murderer known to her, or had he been a stranger? Had he bludgeoned her before he cut her? The crime had begun to stink like vinegar and potash; perhaps like the very mouth of hell. Did sulphur smell something like this? I imagined it must.

I sat with the tip of my pen between my teeth as words began to coalesce, unsummoned, in my mind.

> *In Seven Dials there is a slave*
> *To ink and quill and death...*

I shook them away. What was I thinking? This was a job, and I had to concentrate. I closed my eyes and pictured her, yet when I did, I saw her with someone else's face.

> *A man whose heart is blackened still*
> *With memories of love*

I opened my eyes to see the old wooden box. Had I heard something from within? A rustling of paper, perhaps – or a tapping, very faint, but with an unmistakeable rhythm, by now so familiar: eight, six, eight...

Of course I had not. I returned to the page, where I discovered, scrawled in my hand, a few lonely and disconnected words: *Slut. Streetwalker. Jezebel.*

'Can't say that.' The loud, perfectly reasonable voice startled me so much that a fat ink blot fell from my pen. Behind me, it went on: 'She's a lady, ain't she? It's *'im* you're supposed to patter about.'

It was Briggs, and he was right. I hadn't even been thinking of her, not really. It was another face that was before me, though she did not look like any of those things; she was perhaps a little plain, yet sweet enough and smiling, her cheeks tinted with the daintiest blush.

I returned to my task with renewed vigour. I struck out all that I had done and headed the page anew: *Upon the Wicked Murder of the Beautiful Eliza Seddon in Burlington Place.*

And it *was* wicked. Far more wicked than I had ever been... and here was my chance to begin afresh. Efface all my history. Be made clean again.

New words began to form, overwriting the old. And yet somehow, it was something Briggs said to me that echoed in my mind:

It don't reek... It don't reek when you're mired right in it!

~

No streams of crimson blood did flow
But still her life was fled
As sure as if he took a club
And battered in her head.

I lay awake, rhythms turning and circling in my mind like coins boiling in vinegar. The night was as dark as pitch yet, to my fevered brain, the one who sang and whispered them in my ear was close, a solid presence, his face as clear to me and as evil as the night that would not end.

In Seven Dials there is a slave
To ink and quill and death
A man whose heart is blackened still...

It began over again. I rubbed my eyes and tried once more to fling the visions from me. Now I knew why Peberdy insisted on his eight-six-eight; the rhythm had buried itself into my brain, a beat that was no more escapable than that of life – or death.

Finally, sleep must have come, for the presence was there again, this time standing over me. He was holding an axe, but this time he did not have a face. I peered at him, but all was in shadow except his eyes, and I awoke, sweating and cold, shivering in the pale light of dawn.

I could still hear a voice – and I realised a man was standing beneath my window, selling penny dreadfuls. That brought me back to

myself. People could not afford newspapers –
the duties levied on them had driven prices high
– but murder was sold cheap. With that thought
I began to dress, ready for a day in the Dials,
surrounded by the stench of vinegar and potash
and ink and blood.

I entered the premises of Algernon Peberdy,
Balladeer Nonpareil, went past the destitutes
buying sixpenny bundles, and ascended past
the chatter and rattle of the presses to find the
office empty. The box was there, though, where
it had always been, on the windowsill, basking
in an unlikely little spill of sunlight. It struck me
like a presence, like eyes watching me from the
corner. I sat at the desk but it kept drawing my
gaze, no matter how I resolved not to look upon
it again.

Then the door burst open behind me and
Peberdy himself came in. 'Have you not heard?'
he said, without preliminaries. 'Get to it, lad.
They've only gorn an' nabbed him.'

~

The cove sat silent in the dock
His deeds worse than his lies
And all looked on and each man knew
The meaning of his guise

I painted a picture of guilty conscience, but when
I imagined the murderer, I sensed nothing but
fear. How many times must he have imagined

stepping up to the rope? And yet it is not a hangman I see but a *hexecutioner*, a dark figure holding an axe, his face covered save for his eyes...

My gaze stole once more to the box. I had no intention of looking inside, of searching out the ballad said to be within.

No one can read it, see, without seein' his own black heart reflected there. Then their soul belongs to him – to Jack Ketch – the hexecutioner. Or the Devil, acourse.'

My soul was deeply mired enough already.

It don't reek... It don't reek when you're mired right in it!

But it did. It reeked of vinegar and potash and yes, of sulphur.

I closed my eyes, feeling for a moment the touch of soft fingers brushing my cheek. I shook my head. I hadn't bludgeoned anyone; I hadn't raised a hand. *I love you*, she had said to me. *And I you*, I had answered. I had run my own fingers through her golden hair.

> *The golden stuff spilled o'er his hand*
> *And all his greed was roused...*

The words came as if whispered in my ear. And I saw it: not her hair – *Evangeline, Evangeline's hair* – but coins, overflowing and spilling their golden contents into my hand.

Isn't that what I had sought, truly – the inheritance that was to come, rather than a living, breathing woman?

And yet there had been no coin. Oh, I saw it spilling from her father's hands freely enough, bright, clean coin, but I had discovered his fortune to be entailed to a distant cousin, something she had not thought to tell me while I wooed her – while I kissed her, and she allowed me to kiss her, something she surely ought not have done...

Slut. Street-walker. Jezebel.

I pushed myself up from my chair and went to the window. The taint of bubbling coin was carried on the breeze but the taste was of water, filthy water, and I leaned out, suddenly nauseous. I realised that my fingers had closed about the box, were clinging to it as tightly as a drowning man clutches at a spar. I tried to take a deep draught of air, but choked as the stink flooded in.

> *She looked her last in deep despair*
> *And to the bridge she went*
> *Where all the common harlots leap'd*
> *When their sad lives were spent.*

I roused myself to the sight of Briggs leaning over me, slapping at my cheek. 'What?' I asked him. 'What did you say?' But he only looked puzzled.

> *The slimy stream did wash her clean*
> *Of love and sin alike...*

The whisper wasn't coming from Briggs. It was coming from the window – no, from the box set upon the sill. A hoarse, dry whisper that twisted my insides, that clouded my mind with fear. Words that reeked of sulphur.

I had not bludgeoned her, I told myself. I had simply told her I could not marry her. How could I? I had to seek out coin, to make my way in the world. Surely anyone could see that? All I had done was broken my promise, but Evangeline had broken hers too, hadn't she? She may not have said it in so many words, but she had let me believe her an heiress.

Some smaller, deeper voice within me protested that we had never spoken of such a thing, and I silenced it. She must have *known*. And she had let me peel the sleeves from her arms, releasing each tiny button of her gown—

She *gave* herself to me. Like a slut, I tried to tell myself; like a Jezebel.

And then, just like any common harlot, she had gone to Waterloo Bridge and leaped into the Thames.

She had undone herself, but she had undone me too. My editor was an acquaintance of Evangeline's father, and he must have heard something of it. He had me banished from respectable employment, leaving me poorer than before, and he had done it with that look in his eye; the one I had seen again ranged around the gallery of a courtroom, looking down upon Jem Flitch in the dock.

But he could prove nothing. There could be no sentence...

I shuddered as Briggs slapped my cheek, leaning in so close I could smell the tobacco on his breath. I jerked away in disgust.

'Aye, well that's better, anyhow,' he muttered and stood. 'Thought of all the blood, is it? You'll have ter rid yourself o' that lily liver if you're goin' to keep at this job.'

He nodded towards the verses I had penned, as if they had been the cause of my fit.

I pushed myself up, scowling. What were entrails and spattered brains to me? I was haunted by a plain-featured face with a good smile, by a spill of golden hair, by smooth, whole skin, albeit bloated by the filthy water of the river...

God. I may as well have bludgeoned her. Instead I had killed her so easily, without effort, not like Jem Fitch; without raising my hands, without even shedding a tear. I had killed her with my words.

Now I must write of it all. I must steep my hands in it further, darkening them with ink rather than blood. And so I returned to my task, deserving no better; framing the rhymes, counting the beats. I returned to it with *alacrity*, shutting out the thought of anything and anyone else.

~

The next morning, the crowd outside Newgate was packed so tightly I could scarcely move amid the throng. It was Jem Fitch's turn to hang, and all of gloating humanity had turned out to see it. Those who battened on the gathered crowds were also there in abundance: a man sold bottles of beer from a sack, whilst another attempted to wheel a cart loaded with oranges through the tide. And there, at the foot of the gallows, a woman lifted her voice in song. I could scarcely hear her over the cacophony, but I knew the words anyway. She was a ballad-monger, and the doggerel verse on her lips was mine.

The condemned man stood silent with his head bowed. Everything had been said already; I had written his last words for him.

The hangman stepped forward. I did not stay longer; I tried to tell myself he had not, for a moment, stared directly at me.

I did not return to **Peberdy's** until the afternoon and even then, I did not write a line. Ketch's box was silent; it did not sing to me, not now. It did not need to. The words were inside me. I could not stop hearing them.

Joskins came in and went out. Briggs too, I think. I did not heed them and they did not press me to. I stayed until even the fire in the yard must have died, for the ever-present scent of vinegar began to fade; unless it was that I was becoming accustomed to it at last.

It was only when the light was draining from the sky that I allowed myself to look upon the box again. Somehow, the time had not seemed right until now. Dark deeds required darkness, after all, and I moved towards it, my movements slow, as if wading through deep water.

I reached out and touched the dry wood. Nothing happened; it did not burst into flame, as I had half expected. I picked it up and gently shook it. Something shifted inside: as light or as heavy as a single sheet of paper.

I took it to the desk, opened the drawer and found there a key. I knew it had to be the right one: small and wickedly formed and rusted. I set it to the lock. Despite the rust it fitted perfectly and turned easily, with a sharp little *snick*. I paused then, remembering what I had been told – that if I opened the box, if I read the ballad, I would cast my soul away.

It was suddenly difficult to breathe. I heaved air into my lungs like a man drowning, and threw back the lid.

In Seven Dials there is a slave
To ink and quill and death...

For a moment I saw the words written there, quite plainly, just as I had imagined them; and then I blinked and saw what really lay within. It was a single sheet of parchment, as I had expected, though it was not faded and yellowed with time. This paper was black, as black as my heart, and I stared at it. Was it covered in blood – or ink? Was there really any difference?

I took it into my hands. Despite its age, the paper was damp, though the moisture did not darken my fingers and it did not smell of blood. If anything, it smelled of the river; of the brown, filthy Thames.

Then laughter grated at my back and I turned to see Joskins and Briggs crushed together into the doorway, their faces split with mirthful grins. 'I said!' Briggs let out between gasps. 'I said he'd open it, didn't I?'

Joskins shook his head as he took out a purse, extracted a coin and passed it to his fellow. 'Just cost me an 'alf sovereign,' he said to me.

Briggs bit down on the coin then pocketed it. 'You gave such a fine speech,' he said. 'Where's yer morals now, lad? Where's yer *nobility?*'

I could not reply.

'Never mind,' Briggs went on, his voice scraping inside my mind, 'It don't signify. You can't do this job with a soul anyway lad, eh – not this!'

I simply stared. Soon, I knew, they would retreat to one of the public houses that ringed the centre of the Seven Dials. Briggs would celebrate his gain and Joskins mourn his loss. And I – this time, I thought I would go with them. I too had lost something after all, and there was nothing left to do but see it on its way.

Naturally, I could not do this job with a soul. I think I had always known that: I had heard it in the voice of the woman who sold my words at the gallows' foot. I had seen it in the faces of the wretches who bought them. None of them were looking for redemption. They did not seek caution against following a sinful course, nor did they seek salvation. They wanted blood, only that; they sought to be steeped in it. They craved only more of the depravity into which mankind could sink, and the more dreadful it became, the better they liked it.

I began to smile, remembering the words that had haunted me, the ones I had imagined written by Jack Ketch himself. I remembered my guilt. But the thing that had so haunted me was never my guilt: it was my conscience.

Now it fled from me. For this is who I was, wasn't it? It was my calling to profit from sin. I must delight in blood. I would wallow in the mire as deeply and as long as I was able, and I would be paid for it, in coin as shining and free from the past as I would be.

I replaced the paper in the box – was it really damp, or had that only been my imagination? – and I closed the lid upon their jest. Really, it was rather a fine one. And I took up my coat and proclaimed my readiness to stand them in drink.

They replied with a cheer, clapping me on the back as we started down the stairs. The three of us laughed together. Then Briggs said, 'Course, that's not the real legend of Jack Ketch, anyhow. You don't need no box for that.'

There was something in his words that gave me pause. Or perhaps it was something else; something about the shadows that seemed to coalesce around me, forming and re-forming, like light reflected beneath a bridge; gleaming back from murky water. I suddenly did not wish to take another step.

'It's not the words in a box that'll drive a man mad,' Briggs went on. 'Them's not the ones to worry over. It's the ones he whispers in your ear at night. Oh, he sings a ballad all right, Jack Ketch. But he don't need paper to write it down.'

I opened my mouth, but I could not speak. My throat was dry. I suddenly only wanted to slake it, to plunge into deep water. Briggs' voice had given way to echoes that hung about the stairway, echoes that, like the shadows, seemed to coalesce into something new:

> She took his hand and drew him down
> And held him close about
> Her kiss was all 'twas left for him
> The hangman's claim will out...

'What did you say?' I whispered. I turned about, but I couldn't see Briggs' face any longer, nor Joskins'. There was only a single dark shape that did not reply, that had nothing left to say. I could still feel the rhythm of his verse, however, the beat matching that of my heart. It almost appeared that he was carrying an axe, but in that I must be mistaken, though I knew this was not Briggs, nor Joskins; it was not even Jack Ketch any longer.

A moment later, the foetid reek of sulphur crept towards me. The black shape reached out his hand. I waited for his whisper, to hear his accusation, but he need not say it. There was no ballad to be sung for me; I was beyond words. My deeds did not warrant any. He simply wrapped his cloak around me, and it was dark and soft and choking and as liquid as ink.

The Winter Tree

Miss Lennox. Miss Alexandrina Lennox... I smiled at the thought of her name, perhaps because she had so recently consented to change it, as early as was practicable, to Mrs Arthur Geddes. It was so simple a thing and yet so momentous; my heart alternately leaped and stuttered at the idea of such a decision having been made, and without reference to my father, who had departed this earth some years ago, or my mother, who sadly left it eighteen months past. And yet neither could have withheld their approval, since the lady was of such impeccable taste and breeding, and of course, so very lovely.

My mother's face rose before my mind's eye, pale and stern as she had been since my father's death, driving the smile from my lips. I tried to tell myself that she would share in my joy, at least since she could no longer herself be the presiding angel of my hearth.

Alexandrina now wore my opal ring upon her finely formed hand – her hand that would soon be placed in my own, for ever after. I cast aside all trace of doubt and reminded myself that I was young, and had prospects; I had a beautiful lady who would form the locus of my happiness. What place had doubt in such a world? Even the drab streets of the city must have felt it, for the plane trees were in fresh spring leaf, the sky was if not sunny at least clear of fog and smuts, and the distant sound of some housemaid's singing drifted in snatches through the air. Nothing could spoil such a moment, until I put my hand into my pocket.

I stopped dead at the touch of the unfamiliar and unexpected object I found under my fingers. I knew at once what it was, though I could not have said why. I stood there, the blood draining from my face as I felt the return of all the unwelcome emotions it summoned.

I see everything, Arthur. I am ashamed! How could you be so wicked? To think that a son of mine should bring me to this...

I could not draw breath. I was twelve years old again, standing in my father's study, and tears were pouring down my cheeks. The offending item was held in the outstretched palm of my mother's hand and it was her accusing stare, more than any other thing, which was the most terrible. She thrust it towards me. I knew she wanted me to look upon my misdeed, and I did, and nobody spoke.

It was a little paste brooch, shaped into the semblance of roses and painted in gaudy pinks and yellows. My mother had cast her glance over it in a shop of odds and ends and declared it not worth tuppence. It was priced at two shillings, at which she snorted; she had often declared the proprietor to be a scoundrel, and I happened to have had tuppence in my pocket. It had not seemed so very awful, then, to slide the item into my pocket when no one was looking, and replace it with my little coin.

But my mother's face told me that it *was* awful. It was worse than awful; it had made her unhappy.

'I did not even *like* it, Arthur,' she said, her voice suddenly breaking. 'You know I did not!'

With a start, I realised two things: first, that my mother imagined I had stolen the bauble for her; and second, that my supposed misjudgement of her taste was, to her, more dreadful than the way I had expressed it.

I removed the object from my pocket now and stared at it, and I did not know what to think. It *was* the brooch, just as I had surmised, and it was as poor a thing as I remembered. The paint had chipped a little in the intervening time, but it was otherwise just the same. I simply could not imagine how it had come to be in my pocket. My mother had taken it away after she discovered it in my room, and knowing it was something I could not afford to buy, had soon after accused me. I had supposed it to have been returned to the shop, instead of being given to the one it was intended for: the one with a lovely face and ebony curls; the one I had longed to see smiling upon me. My childhood friend, Emeline.

It was years since I had spoken her name, but it formed so easily once more upon my lips.

I shook my head, rousing myself from my reverie. What had I been thinking? That was all in the past; I had been a child. Now I was set to rush headlong into my future with Alexandrina. I thrust the strange item back into my pocket, wondering what on earth I would do with it. I almost did not like to touch it. It did not feel so much like a brooch as the embodiment of a sin, one that had returned to haunt me, despite the way I had been punished for it. My father had beaten me soundly that day, though somehow the thrashing had hurt less than the expression on my mother's face.

And so the gift intended for the object of my childish adoration had never been given. Even before my mother discovered the item, I had decided I could not hand it to her. I never could have rested easy at the idea of giving so sweet a girl something I had gained in such a fashion, and anyway, its gaudy pinks were no match for the blush of her cheek.

I continued along my way, through streets which suddenly seemed interminably busy. I wove between voluminous crinolines, costermongers and their wares, advertising boards, a fellow hooting upon a tin whistle and the leavings of cabmen's horses. I no longer gained any enjoyment from my walk; I was only anxious to reach home. At last I was at the door of the house I had once shared with my parents and now occupied alone. I proceeded into the drawing room and went directly to the mantelpiece, where I knew I would find my mother's photograph.

It was there as it always was, and yet the sight of it came with a shock. My mother was wearing a black dress – she had remained in mourning long after the death of my father, saying if it was the correct thing for the queen, it was correct for her too – and she stared out at me with eyes that were a little too wide. The same uneasiness arose in me that came whenever I looked upon her photograph. It was undoubtedly her, albeit with a countenance a little too pale, yet it was not her. The eyes, besides being too large, were a shade too dark; but then, they were not her own. Her eyes had already been closed in death when the photographer had come, unspeaking and grim, and arranged her for this memento mori. Now the painted stare of her painted eyes was endless, as if she were looking into eternity itself.

My gaze dropped to the mantel. There, crumpled at the base of the picture, was the little piece of black lace with which I had curtained her image, telling myself it was respectful for the dead as well as more comfortable for the living. At some point during the day – it had not been so this morning – it must have fallen, allowing her to look out upon the world again. I closed my own eyes, though I could not shut out that stare, and I heard her words again as if it were yesterday:

I see everything, Arthur.

I shook away such thoughts, remembering the way I had turned to her for comfort after my father had whipped me. She had shushed me, and wrapped her arms around my thin shoulders. She told me it did not matter, not to her. That she understood. She said that she, of all the women in the world, loved me the most; she promised to be there for me always.

~

Alexandrina stared down at the brooch. At first she looked puzzled and then her expression changed. She tried to cover it with a smile, but it was too late to conceal her flash of disdain. I was at once irritated and repentant. I had wished to do something with the item – after all, it had been returned to me, surely to some purpose – and it had felt, at the moment of giving, imbued with every suitable emotion: adulation; hope; even love. Now I saw that I had been foolish. The brooch was connected only with contempt and sorrow, all wrapped in a tawdry, chipped scrap of paste. It was nothing but the gift of a child to a child, and so it should have remained.

Still, Alexandrina smiled uncertainly, pinned it to her cape and took my arm. I tried to banish it from my mind, already hoping that she would never wear it again. I should have no doubt of that, of course. So poor a thing did not suit her. Alexandrina had been named for our good Queen Victoria, although our monarch had chosen to eschew her first given name and call herself by her second; and queenly she was. Her bearing was straight as we proceeded into the park towards the bandstand, where, it being a Saturday, a brass band merrily played. We spoke of this and that as we stood with the crowd that had gathered there, the ladies needlessly yet fashionably shading their faces with bright parasols. Pretty indeed they looked against the lawn, which sloped away to an ornamental stretch of water, where the more energetic gentlemen rowed their ladies about in little wooden boats.

It was all thoroughly charming, and yet somehow I could not help comparing it in my mind's eye with another walk on a different day, so that I almost thought I heard high, tinkling laughter floating on the air. I closed my eyes. Emeline had been older then, and I saw the graceful wave of her hand as she whirled about a tree as if it were a partner in a dance. I saw again the gleam of her hair, the sway of her dress. She had blossomed like springtime, though her skirts were darkened at the hem by the snow which lay all about us.

I gave a wistful smile. I recalled it all so clearly. That day had been some years after I had thought of giving Emeline the brooch, though I had not yet come of age. Our families had been close by; my father was acquainted with hers through his business, though her parent was not so successful as my own. Still, we had often been thrown together, Emeline and I, though our elders had stayed by the walk whilst we were concealed by the white undulations of the ground.

She took hold of a branch above her head and shook loose a scattering of snowflakes, which settled upon her shoulders and caught in her eyelashes. 'Do you see it?' she asked. And I almost thought I had, though I did not altogether know what she meant.

'I shall always think of you when I am here,' she said. 'And in my mind it shall always be just as it is today.'

I do not know what I replied.

'The winter tree,' she proclaimed. 'That is its name, now.'

No. I must not think of that. It was past, but although Alexandrina touched my hand with her gloved fingers, I could not help dwelling on Emeline. I had given her nothing, not even that ill-formed brooch, and she had never complained to me, not once. And it occurred to me that I could see her again. My mother had been determined that I should drop the association, but now there was no disapproving parent to stand in my way. I could go to her if I wished.

'Isn't this wonderful?'

Alexandrina's voice intruded on my thoughts, calling me back to the present. She did not look as if she thought it wonderful. She patted my hand once more and I realised she had noticed my distraction. I made some remark on the music and offered to bring her a little refreshment. She looked brighter at that, and I slipped my hand into my pocket to find some coin, starting when something jabbed into my fingertip.

'Whatever is the matter?' she said.

'Nothing, my dear,' I replied, unfortunately at that moment removing my hand to reveal the pale grey kid of my glove crimsoned with a drop of blood.

'Do let me see.'

'Really, it is nothing.' I forced a smile, slipping my hand into my pocket again, feeling more cautiously its contents. I thought I knew what had caused the injury, or suspected, and I was determined that Alexandrina should not see it. The thought of its being there, inexplicable and undeniable, filled me with wonder and dismay. How? First the brooch and now this – it was impossible!

'Allow me to help you.' Alexandrina reached for my arm and I whipped my hand from my pocket once more.

'It was a pin, my dear – only a pin. I must have words with my tailor.' I forced myself to speak with jollity.

'Or your laundress. That jacket surely is not new, is it, Arthur?'

I ignored the note of contempt that had stolen into her voice. I knew she had not meant it, and was relieved when she did not press me further. Still, my hand kept creeping towards my pocket as we finished our meanderings. Finally we parted and I turned towards home. I still had not looked at the object I had found. I did not need to. I could picture it perfectly: a hatpin, silver and sharp, adorned with the carving of a leaf. The leaf was of oak, the same kind of tree we had stood beneath the day Emeline had given it to me, though its branches had been bare then. And I remembered, in spite of myself, the words she had spoken when she removed it and pinned it to my jacket.

I shall never love anyone else, Arthur. I shall never marry anybody but you.

I had placed my hand over it, holding it to my heart. Later, I had secreted it in my room – indeed, for a while, I hid it beneath my pillow – until one day it was gone, and I never found it again. I assumed that the maid had discovered it there, and thinking it misplaced, had put it with my mother's things. I did not dare ask after it.

But the next evening, my mother spoke to me of Emeline. She said the girl was forward; that she was vain. She said she held ideas above her station. I had not known how to reply or where to look. She said that Emeline would surely turn out to be a harridan, and just for a moment, I had wondered if it was true. I think that was the end of it for us; the seed had been planted. Not long afterwards, I heeded my mother's advice and cast Emeline aside.

~

As soon as I reached home, I hurried to see my mother's photograph. I had clothed it again in its curtain of lace, but I was unsurprised to see it had fallen once more to the mantel and that her eyes were endlessly staring out at me. What did surprise me, though, was the expression in those painted orbs. Her visage was as cold and lifeless as ever, but was it only my imagination that her eyes had changed – that they were filled, now, with something resembling regret?

~

It did nothing to dispel the tendency of my thoughts when, upon next seeing my betrothed, she announced an intention of riding out in a carriage and driving around the park. I tried to scotch the notion, but her face fell and her lip trembled. It was the return of her little frown, though, the one that said, *I do not know why you should behave so*, that made me alter my demeanour and smile my approval.

We discussed small matters of the wedding, in which I concurred with all her pretty wishes, not wanting to think too deeply upon the matter of orange blossom or rose petals; and so it was strange to me that, if anything, her manner became more agitated as we went. We stepped from the carriage and walked a little, though I did not notice which way we wound through the flowerbeds and lawns, letting it all become a blur in my sight. The sun was trying, if somewhat weakly, to penetrate the cloud, and parasols once again held sway over umbrellas.

Alexandrina's voice broke into my thoughts. 'In my mind,' she said, 'it shall always be just as it is today.'

I turned to her, suddenly cold. 'I beg your pardon?'

'Arthur,' she said, 'you do not listen.'

'Of course I do, my sweet.'

'I shall always think of you when I am here,' she said.

The blood drained from my cheeks.

'Arthur, whatever is the matter? You are distracted. I knew that you were distracted.'

'Not so, my dear.'

'Well, then – do you see it?'

I could do nothing but gawp at her words. Alexandrina drew a heavy sigh and raised her gaze to the heavens. I looked for the first time at what lay about me, already knowing what I would see. We had progressed beyond the gates and the busier drives; we had left the bustle of society behind us. Instead, wherever I looked, there was verdure. And there, at the heart of it, was a slope I recognised. Between it and where we stood was an oak tree. It was clothed in springtime green, leaves quivering in the breeze, but still I knew that it was *our* tree: the winter tree. It was not winter now of course, yet for a moment I saw its branches laden with snow, everything blanketed in white save for the marks our footsteps had made around its trunk. And I heard again the words she had spoken:

'I shall love anyone else, Arthur.'

I looked at Alexandrina, who frowned at my astonishment, as if she did not know what could be the matter.

I shall never marry anybody but you.

I gave a little cry and walked away from her, making some gesture of apology or perhaps repudiation. I did not look back and did not look at the tree again, not then. I did not know what was happening or why Alexandrina should have spoken those words to me. How could she possibly have *known*? Emeline and I had been alone together.

Had she even spoken them at all?

I came to myself, realising I had left my fiancé standing alone in the middle of the park. I turned again but could not see her; when I looked towards the drive, I could not see our carriage either. Alexandrina had not waited and I did not blame her for an instant.

Before I left, I turned and looked upon the winter tree. I half expected to see it as it had been in memory, but of course I did not. It was only a tree, and there was no one standing beneath its branches. Its colours were almost drab against the dullness of the day.

I walked to the edge of the park and hailed a hansom cab. I meant to direct the driver to the home of my intended, but instead found myself giving my own address. I did not know why, except that some part of me longed for dark rooms and quietness and counsel, and then I realised there would be no counsel, that I would be alone.

Unless the veil has fallen once more from my mother's eyes.

I pushed the thought away. My hand shook as I paid the driver and alighted at my door. I could not order the tumult in my mind nor calm my spirit. It felt as if the world was rushing towards some crisis, one that I had always known must happen.

I shall never marry anybody but you.

Nor I you, Emeline.

I pressed my eyes closed with my fists. What had I done?

I had made a promise to Alexandrina. It was not possible that I could go back on my word – and yet, had I not already done such a thing? Now it seemed that not only did my own soul cry out against it, but that of my mother, who had been the instrument of our parting. Was she showing her regret from beyond the grave – had she found a way? The brooch and the hatpin had been in her possession, and now they called my attention to the sin I had committed, with my prevarication and hesitation, my inconstancy—

I plunged my hand into my pocket, pressing my fingers into each corner. Now, when I needed it most of all, there was nothing there, no message from the past. A wave of despair came over me and I blinked rapidly as I entered the hall, nodding to the servant as she took my coat. I proceeded into the drawing room.

There, on the mantelpiece, was my mother's photograph. She was looking out at me again, and yet she no longer stared. She met my eye with a look brim-full of sympathy. And there, hanging over her, in a vase which had hitherto been empty, was a single twig of oak; it bore only a few scant shrivelled leaves, but was covered to the tip in pale and glistening ice.

~

My hand shook as I wrote, the words appearing wavering and uncertain even whilst my determination grew. I kept glancing at the twig from the winter tree. As my feelings poured onto the sheet of paper, droplets of water formed along its fringe of ice and dripped to the mantel. A part of me desperately wished to hold onto it, to preserve it just as it was, but I had no means of doing so. If I tried to cling to it the heat from my hands would destroy it all the faster; I could only watch as it melted.

I forced myself to write more quickly. The idea had come upon me that I must finish my letter before the ice was gone, though I knew not why; I only knew that these strange messages had come to me, and the letter must be sent before my resolution failed.

I scarcely knew what I wrote. I spoke of remorse, certainly. I spoke of sorrow. I spoke of the wrongness of seeking her hand when I had what could only be considered a prior engagement, albeit one that had been formed before the idea had taken on the seriousness it deserved in my mind. I said she must consider herself free of all ties, that she should rejoice to be rid of one so unworthy. I pictured her reading it, her eyes widening, the withheld breath and the curl of her lip; I saw her contempt. I comforted myself with the notion that she would not be hurt so very deeply. Indeed, she would recognise that it was the right thing; she must. Our love could never mean so much as the one from the past. How could it? My love for Emeline and hers for me had reached across the years. My mother had shown me that, crossing the misty veil to bring us together once more, to right what had surely been a great wrong. She was doing everything in her power to secure my happiness – could any mortal man ignore such a thing? I had treated Alexandrina abominably, but she would rise above it. The smaller wrong must give way before the greater.

I signed the letter, folded it and called the maid, bidding her to have it delivered within the hour. It was done; I could not now, in some momentary weakness, change my mind. My intentions made clear, free to do what I always should have done, I sat back and breathed in deeply. My glance went to the winter tree. The ice was gone; in its place was nothing more than a bare and skeletal twig.

~

My servant must have carried out my instructions with alacrity, for as I left the house a cab drew to a halt a little farther along the road. With dismay, I saw my erstwhile fiancée alighting from it. My heart sank further when I made her out. Her hair was covered by nothing more than an indoors piece of lace, and she wore no coat; her shawl hung loose from one arm, trailing in the filth at the side of the road. Yet all of that was nothing beside her expression.

Alexandrina was so ghastly pale, for a moment I imagined her a corpse. Her eyes belied that impression, however, flashing with greater intensity than I had ever seen in her.

'You – you!' she cried. Her shawl fell as she strode towards me and I did not move to retrieve it. I could only stare. I had not suspected her of such depth of feeling. I realised I had not suspected her of love.

I opened my mouth to murmur some apology – I scarcely knew what words I spoke – but it was of no use, for she showed no sign of hearing them. She stretched out her hand and I waited for her exclamation, but she did not speak, and I realised she was showing me something: my ring, still encircling her finger.

I glanced around. Passers-by had stopped in the street and were staring, even the urchin of a crossing-sweeper at the corner. I opened my mouth to ask her not to shame us both, but was transfixed by the brilliance of her eyes.

'Why?' she demanded. 'What did I do to deserve such treatment – to be thrown over in such a fashion? To be made an object of ridicule, and scorn, and – *pity!*'

I did pity her, but my urge to recant, to take back my letter and burn it, was quelled by the remembrance of my mother's look; fixed on me, bidding me do the right thing.

'Forgive me,' I said, 'please.' A distant part of me, or perhaps an echo of my mother's voice, thought to tell her that she need not become an object of ridicule if she did not make herself one; but I swallowed down the words.

'I should not have proposed marriage to you,' I said. 'I was sworn to another, though it had long since been swept aside, as should not have been. Now I must make amends.'

'To *her* – to some other woman? Not to me?'

'I wish I could, Alexandrina.'

'Do not call me that!'

'I am truly sorry – Miss Lennox.' I gave a slight bow, to which she responded by straightening and assuming a haughty look, as if recalled to the knowledge of her moral superiority.

'And who is this lady, for whom I am so casually flung aside?'

I suddenly did not wish to answer. I did not want to bandy Emeline's name in the street for it to be sullied with insults. But my lips formed the word so easily, as if it was a natural thing. 'It is Miss Emeline Harris.'

Alexandrina caught her breath and her lip twitched, I thought with pain, but then she only looked puzzled. 'You jest,' she said softly. 'You abandon me, exposing me to the censure of the world, and now you prank at my expense?'

'Of course I would not.'

'Then why,' she said, her expression hardening, 'do you toy with me so? Or have you lost your sanity as well as your honour?'

My cheeks reddened. How could she accuse me, after chasing after me in the street, acting the Bedlamite herself? I had to swallow down the retort that rose to my lips. I reminded myself I had wronged her, had been unfeeling, but still I had no reply to offer.

'It is true, then?' she said, her lips bloodless, and she drew in a deep breath. 'You have jilted me and treated me so, all for the memory of a dead girl?'

The world stopped. I could not decipher her meaning and yet it worked its way to my heart, turning to a shard of ice. She threw back her head and laughed. That, of all things, I could not bear to see: the look upon her face. The delight. I could not bear that I had caused her to hate me so utterly, and yet I deserved it; I knew that I did.

Emeline – dead? It was impossible. She had always been so full of life. She still was, whenever I closed my eyes. I shook my head. 'I would know of it,' I said. 'We are no longer acquainted as we once were, it is true, but I would have heard of such a thing. I would have attended her funeral.'

'Ha!' She replied. 'A funeral – could she have expected one, do you imagine? And do you think anyone would have spoken of it so openly – of what she did? Of course they could not.'

I stared. 'Whatever do you mean?'

'Her sin! The worst one of all. For heaven's sake – it was your own mother who told of it to mine. It reached their ears, no matter how her family wished it hushed up. I overheard them gossiping of it at tea. The girl did it to herself. She took her own life.'

I mouthed my denial that such a thing was possible, though I could not speak.

Alexandrina smiled her triumph. 'There could be no funeral,' she said, 'for very shame. I do not even know where they would have buried her. A crossroads perhaps, or some unhallowed spot, with a stake through her heart.'

I let out a cry of anguish.

'I know how she did it, though,' she went on, 'if you wish to hear it. She drank lye – a terrible way to perish, by all accounts. She did not even have the decency to do it in secrecy, but took it and drank it in the park, where anyone could find her—'

She had not finished, and called something after me, but I could not make out the words. I was already hurrying away; I knew exactly where I must go.

~

A short time later, I stood beneath the winter tree. I let my head fall back and peered up through its branches, remembering. I could still see the graceful twirl of Emeline's hand in the movement of the leaves, but of course, back then, there had been no leaves. Now they shifted from silver to green to grey as they turned in the breeze. I could smell the green rawness of spring, the rising sap, the potency of the earth beneath my feet. Everything about me was blossoming anew – but not her. I looked down at the base of the tree, almost glimpsing for a moment a pale shape clad in a thin dress, writhing in her agonies. How could she have done it? And yet I heard her answer, whispering in the leaves:

I shall never love anyone else, Arthur. I shall never marry anybody but you.

I hid my face in my hands. How could I have let her go? Now she was so very near, yet parted from me by an impossible distance.

This tree should be clothed in winter. It should have remained so for ever, in memory of her. Still, I could feel the cold of it: a shard of ice twisting deeper into my heart, the chill spreading slowly outward. It followed my veins, tracing each sinew, finding smaller and smaller pathways until my cheeks and fingers grew as numb as my feelings. I remembered the way she had declared her love, so open, so certain of my response, and the cold within me burned. Had Emeline burned too? What must she have felt, as the caustic stuff poured down her throat, eating away her very soul?

For heaven's sake – it was your own mother who told of it to mine...

I turned and stumbled away. I could not bear it, could not think any longer. I do not know where I went or what I did, until I found myself at home, in the drawing room, standing before my mother's picture.

The black curtain had fallen from the photograph; she had cast it off. She stared out at me and I stared back, until her eyes were the only things in existence. They had turned cold again, watching me, judging me. In the next moment, I had caught up the picture and dashed it into the fireplace. Glass shattered, shards glistening like ice. I teased the photograph free of its frame, then ran my fingertips across the smooth paper until I felt the dryness of paint.

I set my fingernails against her eyes and scratched. Paint – that was all they were. It was not possible that her expression could have changed. Now the paint flaked from the picture and I saw my mother's eyes – her true eyes. They were blank and closed and unseeing. Dead eyes in a dead face; that was all they had ever been.

And yet I could feel her gaze on me still.

I shall never marry anybody but you, Emeline had said.

And I had replied: *Nor I you, Emeline.*

I knew, now, that those words were true. I could never marry. I would never be permitted to marry. There could only ever be one presiding angel of my hearth, and she had never left it. Even death had not taken her from me, and here was proof: the cold of it was buried in my bones and beneath my skin, a winter tree icing each vein, encasing each nerve, seizing each limb in an iron grip. This ice would never melt; the spring would not come to thaw it. I would never be free of it. I deserved no better.

I closed my eyes and saw behind them my mother, looking back at me. Of all the women in the world, she was the one who loved me the most; the one who had promised to be there for me always.

The Flowering

Afterwards, I cannot help thinking of her. I am supposed to be setting down in my notes a description of some new cultivars, which my master, Mr Petherton, shall put into his catalogue. It is easy work in comparison to digging the flowerbeds and the constant vigilance against weeds, and I am grateful to be entrusted with it. And yet I read again what I have written: *Growing to a height of about two feet, with clusters of small flowers, white, pink, or violet, and pale fronds about the eyes...*

My pen has run on with my memories, and I strike out the last word, an unaccustomed blot on my work. I do not write the things that continue to run through my mind: *Hair of gold gathered into fantastical gleaming twists, skin of blameless white, and yes, those eyelashes, appearing like white fronds in the morning sun; the dress, simple and blameless likewise, all the graceful adornment she requires, and in her hands...*

I remember what happened yesterday and frown. My master and I had dressed so carefully,

Mr Petherton donning his fur-trimmed gown and chains before calling for a carriage to take us to St Giles Without Cripplegate, that ancient church so beloved of the Worshipful Company of Gardeners. I had helped him alight and stood by as the Company processed towards the altar in pairs, carrying their ceremonial silver spade, before we took our places for the Fairchild Sermon.

A glory of light set the windows ablaze in brilliant reds and blues. The pews were full, the choir in good voice, and there was only the faintest smell of dust, which must have arisen from the church, since I had thoroughly scrubbed the soil from under my nails.

Then I twisted in my seat and saw her: Millicent Ashton, the luxuriant fronds of her eyelashes resting on her cheek, since her face was demurely downcast. I could still see their loveliness, however, as the priest stepped to his lectern and any last shuffling and whispering ceased.

The priest spoke of creation. He spoke of the third day, when God called forth every single herb and grass and fruit-bearing tree, fixed and unchanging, for ever and ever, amen. He spoke of the wondrous variety that was then called into being, the fecundity which Adam would have the pleasure of naming. He spoke, in short, of the wonderful works of God in His creation, which was no surprise, since that was what he'd been paid to do. And all throughout his droning twaddle I could not help but glance towards Millicent Ashton and finger the little flowering plant I held in my hand: the one that proved the Company hypocrites and the priest an oaf; the one that gave the lie to it all.

Thomas Fairchild, the patron of this sermon, was also the originator of the first man-made hybrid flower. He was the nurseryman who birthed a flood of new creation, new life and new colour, blooms of which the Creator never dreamed. I turned the flowers in my hand, white and pink, pink and white. I pictured Fairchild labouring over its parent plants, first drawing a feather across the stamen of a sweet William, back and forth, before setting it to the stigma of a carnation, up and down, and sitting back, satisfied, leaving the rest to nature. Waiting as the pollen impregnated the ovule, creating a seed hitherto never seen; as it grew, becoming something new under the sun; as it unfurled, living proof of the sexual reproduction of plants.

Then, shocked at his own audacity, he declared to the Royal Society that it was created by 'serendipity'. Chastened by his blasphemy, he bequeathed the sum of £25 for this sermon to be preached and droned and rattled out annually forever, God bless his fearful little soul, if indeed he possessed such a thing; if do we all.

And the wondrous title of this wonderful specimen? Why, nothing grander than Fairchild's Mule, the same flower I held in my somewhat damp fingers in these latter days of the nineteenth century, over a hundred and fifty years later.

I smirked at the sight of Millicent Ashton's father, that rich old bearded Billy goat, sitting next to his daughter, a ramrod up his back. He could scarcely decline such a specimen on her behalf, not on such an occasion. It was surely of too great an interest to a botanist such as he, albeit he pursues that interest in a respectably amateur way.

I pictured her wearing my little gift, taking it to her room, turning it in her hands. I had made it a habit to present her with little samples for her flower press, on her visits to the nursery; she follows her father in his interest, in an even more amateur way, naturally, and I liked to think of it – her fingers wrapped around their seed heads, tasting their nectar, touching their fruit to her lips.

I shifted in my seat at the image, fixing my eyes on the cadaverous face of the priest, surely enough to cool anyone's ardour. Then I followed my master, filing outside into a day bright with sunlight, holding the Mule – only a little marred with moisture from my hands – to see Millicent Ashton talking and laughing with a fellow I had never seen before.

My consternation was in no way alleviated when my master, upon seeing him, called out a greeting, his hoarse old voice suddenly bright. 'Mr Andrew Nicholls, as I live and breathe! How splendid!'

The young man turned.

'And such a pleasure to see that you are making the acquaintance of the daughter of my most esteemed patron.'

It was neither a pleasure nor especially splendid to see the fellow turn and smile. I would have wished him to have teeth rotting in his head, skin ravaged by the pox, or indeed his whole self to the Devil, rather than in the company of Miss Ashton; but I gave a stiff-jawed smile and followed Mr Petherton, who went towards him and, rather than shaking his hand, enfolded him in his arms.

After more earnest declarations of pleasure, and oddly, apologies on behalf of the young man for not being able to come sooner, my master remembered my presence.

'Do meet my faithful assistant, he said. 'Simon Smith.'

Damn the man, I had to shake his hand, only then remembering the Mule, which had slipped from my fingers. How could I present it to her now? It was sullied; it was ruined. I could not even lift my eyes to her face. I did not wish to see the glow in hers, or how those fronds had been set all a-flutter by this fresh young breeze. I simply placed one foot over the fallen hybrid, as coy as Fairchild himself when he requested this sermon to be preached, as I heard Petherton say the words that put a chill into my heart.

'This is my second cousin's boy,' he said. 'A great surprise for you, I think, Simon! Though it could hardly be otherwise, as I am certain anyone could predict. He is soon to be coming to work with us.'

He clapped the youth on the shoulder. If it were not too obvious to state, too simple to *predict*, I was utterly wordless.

~

All I remember of my mother was walking through Regent's Park, so long ago, holding her hand as she told me of the trees interlacing over our heads and the occasional wild flower that had somehow managed to thrive amid the grass. I remember her gentle looks as she taught me of them all. My mother loved me. She adored me. She would have given me the world; little wonder, then, if her last act in this life was to apprentice me to a man who grew every kind of flower within it.

Perhaps I exaggerate, but so Mr Petherton's nursery had appeared to my young eyes, and if he had not yet obtained every single flower, he was at least avid in trying to fill the deficiency.

Now he wandered with me between the raised beds and trays and pots, demonstrating all the means by which man could overcome nature. He showed me the glass- and hothouses that could give rise to new flowers, both in their season and without, as was required. He offered up all the plants and gave me their names: not those devised by Adam, but the binomial names given by Carl Linnaeus, that great systematiser and scientist of the last century, who categorised plants according to their number of stamens and pistils.

Mr Petherton did not hold my hand, but he had often said he valued me as a son, and stood as a father to me, and he was besides old and without an heir, and who in my place would not imagine...?

For Petherton, too, has flirted with hybrids. The place is seething with their unnatural colours and fantastical forms. And it seemed by no means out of the question that he might one day wish to see a baser scion grafted to a nobler stock – to mangle the words of Shakespeare – for the pleasure of seeing what would become of that.

Now there is this interloper, this popinjay, this distant cousin's son, blue of eye, blonde of hair, bright of smile, hideous; hideous. As I watch, he gestures across the geraniums as if he birthed them all himself, and Miss Ashton, who walks at his side, simpers at his wisdom.

I curse to see him so, strutting about the place like a coxcomb, as if he already owns it all, while I, who reared so many of these jewels from seed, am entirely forgotten. Mr Petherton walks behind them, talking with Mr Ashton, who nods along as sage as Solomon. In their full view, Adam in his Paradise stoops and selects a flower here, a herb there, and snip, snip, gathers them for her. I cannot prevent a snort of laughter. A herb, a twig of evergreen? She has seen them all, many times. Even Linnaeus knew that botany was not opaque to the gentler sex; his system was so simple, he had declared it could even be understood by a woman.

Why, then, does the fool imagine that these commonplaces will fascinate her? Yet she lowers her head as he presents his gift, the better to breathe it in, and looks up at him through those eyelashes.

They take a turn about the rose bushes until they are close by, walking past me without a word.

'Ah, yes,' Petherton is saying to her father, 'I dare say that should be of interest. It is in my special hothouse – it is not, as you know, for everyone. The scent is quite – overwhelming.'

I know at once that they are speaking of one of his special rarities, now in its finest hour: the stinkhorn, or as Linnaeus had proudly named it, the *phallus impudicus*. It could be said that that gentleman was, on occasion, a little injudicious when it came to his naming; one more reason, I suppose, why his publications were somewhat gloriously placed on the Vatican's list of forbidden books.

Still, I wonder that Mr Petherton should mention it within his patron's daughter's hearing. I suggested only a week ago that we should enter the smallest of the hothouses and observe its growth, only for Mr Petherton to answer, in scandalised tones, that perhaps it was a little inappropriate.

I picture it: not a flower or a tree, but a fungus of splendid proportions. The stinkhorn begins its life as an egg. As it develops, the fertile part is thrust upward on a single fleshy stalk of prodigious girth. The deliquescent, gelatinous mass containing its spores, known as the gleba, is enclosed by a membranous cap. The characteristic foul smell is designed to attract *hymenoptera*, the insects which are the instrument for the spores' dispersal.

Now, together, they make their way to gaze upon the *phallus*. Millicent still has her head lowered as she lifts her white skirts, to avoid soiling them on a bed of fine tilth. The father makes no demur. It seems that what was objectionable to look upon with me as their guide is no obstacle with young Master Nicholls at their side.

They emerge a little later, Miss Ashton flushed and pressing Andrew's posy to her nose, as if he had presented it to her for just such a purpose; Mr Petherton smiling at his – *my* – expertise in raising such a beast; Mr Ashton, smiling over his daughter's blushes; and the popinjay, who holds out his arm for her to take. As he does, I notice a book tucked into his pocket.

It does nothing to improve my temper to see, as they take their leave, its title: *Flower Lore: the Teachings of Flowers, Historical, Legendary, Poetical and Symbolic*, by Miss Carruthers of Inverness, where I should very much prefer her silly notions had remained. It is a floral dictionary, wherein, among other nonsense, is to be found a key to the language of flowers, those secret messages passed between lovers, encapsulated in the form of various blooms. He tilts it towards her as she leaves, and I see the nod of understanding she gives him in return.

I think again of the posy he presented to her. Lily-of-the-valley: that, I believe, in the terms of his floriography, is for sweetness and purity. There is lavender, for devotion. Marjoram is for happiness and finally, pricking or not, there is holly: for hope.

In his slovenly, imprecise, girlish breed of language, he speaks to her of love.

~

I am gathering the flora that Mr Ashton has ordered to be sent to his home in the country: great shrubs and saplings, carefully planted and tended and watered by my hand, are now uprooted by my spade. I am digging, in fact, like a peasant, of no more notice than the seagulls with clipped wings that Petherton keeps to peck at snails before they can damage his leaves.

I wipe sweat from my forehead before wrapping a root ball in linen and placing it carefully into a box so that not a hair shall be crushed. In the glasshouse, I can see Andrew – or Adam as I prefer to think of him, this man who seemed to spring into being as suddenly as his namesake, who enjoys this Paradise of another's making. Indeed, he is harvesting the work of my hands. He has no spade, not even a trowel. He snip-snips with a little pair of silver scissors, tilting his head this way and that.

I think of Millicent Ashton: the way she has been tended, watched over, nurtured. She has no siblings, no rival in her blooming. She is lovely; magnificent. Furthermore, she is a perennial, for she alone is to inherit her father's fortune.

I had thought, once I had the nursery, I would have the girl too. Now, like a sunflower, she has turned her face towards a brighter light, as do we all. I watch as Adam arranges the second order placed by the Ashtons, this one of blooms intended to adorn their townhouse, where they currently reside, this being the correct season for the City.

He pauses, bows his head, considers. Then he begins on an arrangement they did not order: a womanish little nosegay wrapped in a paper doily. But of course it is womanish, I realise, as he makes his choice. White jasmine: that's for sweet love. A white rose: purity. And chamomile for patience. He wraps it about with honeysuckle for the bonds of affection, ties it with a silken ribbon and slips it into the case intended for her drawing room. I do not suppose it will reach so far. I imagine her pressing it to her bosom, slipping away with it to her chamber, where it will fragrance the air with the thought of him.

I close my hands into fists. The popinjay sends her such chaste blooms: surely his bed will be every bit as cold.

The father, perhaps I mentioned, is an Enthusiast. He relishes new specimens, the finest examples of which he uses to adorn his carriageway, so that the world may see and admire. His country residence is his hobby; the townhouse, for now, is his home, and cut flowers are essential. They are born and die to decorate his halls, to freshen the air he breathes, to provide a frame for his daughter's loveliness. I wonder if he is something of a Quaker? There is certainly a touch of it about him. The plain way of dressing, the upright stance... I imagine him standing back from my arrangements in sublime contemplation, glorying in God's creation; flowers as a path to the Almighty.

And there they shall be, an extravagant efflorescence. Even Adam nods with admiration when he sees what I have gathered for them today, but he cannot read my language, not yet. For mine is that of true botany – a language that any could understand, if they should only look.

Linnaeus categorised them all by their lascivious nature. The lilies, he said, each frolic with six husbands. The tulips – late bloomers these, but I have coaxed them – are pleasured by upwards of twenty males in a single marriage. And there are marigolds, profligate fellows who dwell not only with numerous wives but concubines too.

I picture Mr Ashton running his hands over my exotic blooms, each displaying their flamboyant wares like a harlot on a street corner, raising their skirts to exhibit their parts; every flower a beautifully curtained and scented bed.

Well, was Linnaeus made of stone? Not for nothing was his taxonomy known as a Sexual System. Plants were arranged into classes and orders by the number of male and female genitalia, while other parts were compared to the labia minora and majora. Little wonder if his obsession spilled over into his descriptions; the language of flowers is not coy, not something to be found between Miss Carruthers' pages but rather between her legs. This is the man who termed the calyx the lips of the cunt; the one who named the impudent phallus. Rousseau once declared that the study of nature could help prevent the tumults of passion; I say Rousseau was a donkey.

And here comes Adam, the innocent fool, dreaming of his Eden. He is holding something in his hands: ah, his little message for his sweet dove. His posy has mint, for virtue; I smell that at once. The red salvia means forever mine, a little florid in its hue, that, but no matter. Likewise the carnations, which signify admiration. The white clover is a mere fodder plant, but its meaning? Think of me.

I stand back and pretend not to notice as he slips it into the box with the rest, and he stands back, though I am certain he listens as I clatter the lid into place and secure the straps. He is already picturing it in her hands, I am certain.

It is good that his back is turned, for I cannot entirely conceal a smile.

Later, I open the box again. I remove the popinjay's tussie-mussie, rip away its ribbon, scatter his sighed-over gifts across the floor. And I take out the choices I have made, arrange them, touch them, tease them, and bind them with his ribbon.

First there is bladder senna, a plant first grown on these shores by Fairchild himself, the swollen pink fruit of which resembles pursed and ready lips. Then there is the arum lily, a rarity: this specimen is known as red desire, a shapely, maidenly white bloom, its sweet cup enclosing a thrusting crimson spadix. Then, in case the message is not sufficiently clear, there is the *clitoria ternatea*, another name sprung from the salacious mind of our revered mentor, the term so obviously suggested by the soft, sensuous folds of flesh-like petals, leading inward to a secret, blushing centre.

I stare at it and reconsider. I look down at the flowers scattered on the floor. I have trampled on Adam's mint; its sharp stink hangs in the air. But there should be a little something of him in this gift, should there not? I stoop, pick up the salvia, strip some of the petals and scatter them among the rest like bright drops of blood.

Still, I am not finished. Before I seal the box again, and ready the sixpence that will ensure my delivery does not arrive until after Mr Ashton returns home from his business, I perfect my arrangement. I straighten the little posy, ensuring that my final touches are positioned at the very front: camellia, representing a gift that has been given to a man; and sweet pea, for pleasures taken, for deepest gratitude; for goodbye.

~

Outrage. Horror. Success! Ashton could not have failed to detect something of my meaning, but it proceeded better than I had hoped. He was so scandalised I ought to have heard the outcry all the way to the glasshouses, though of course I did not. Still, it was enough to hear Mr Petherton's words to Adam, albeit so spluttered and full of spittle and wind he could scarcely get them out.

The bags are packed; the invasive seed is ousted; the innocent corrupted – and I used God's own creation to do it.

I can barely keep from laughing as Adam's conveyance pulls away from the door. He will go back to his second, third or whatever cousin, I suppose, in disgrace and shame. He will benefit from being a little chastened, I think. I can already picture his eyes growing dull over his recollections, his thwarted joys, his disappointed ambitions, but I straighten my face for Mr Petherton is coming down the path, leaning on his stick more heavily than hitherto. He is aimless, now; meandering. *It will not be long*, I think.

Still, I wonder if this expulsion of the upstart weed will be enough to salve Ashton's wound? Indeed, that is something I am long in pondering.

'Twould be a pity if word of his daughter's ruin were to spread, would it not? And he so proud, so very upstanding, such a pillar of the community. I suppose, with the suspicion cast about that his little bloom is already spoiled, he may be rather less averse to an alternative suit. He could scarcely object any longer to the prospect of infecting his family's fine roots with a little wilder stock.

~

After the marriage: bruised stems. Crushed calyx. Torn petals, dampened fronds. Purpled and broken lips.

A pluck'd flower so very quickly begins to wilt.

~

I throw back my head and straighten my spine and walk ahead of Mr Nicholls along the path. There is nothing for him to do but follow, since I am more learned in his business than himself; and he cannot cross so great a patron.

Ah, there was a time when I had hoped that my Adam would be disinherited as well as cast out, but it seems that Petherton could not go so far. And so he has come back again; still, being wrong can bring some fine compensations. I throw open the door to the hothouse and step into the hot stink of overblown flesh. I can tell at once that it is ripe once more; I hear the lazy buzz of flies somewhere among the leaves. However, it is not the shrubs I seek. I step forward until I am standing before the stinkhorn and, with little choice, Adam waits at my side. We contemplate its thrusting glory, its fecund cap. I find I am smiling, though more at the memory of my own restraint than the view. I had been so very tempted to place it at the centre of my rather dramatically effective bouquet; now I am glad I did not. Petherton would almost certainly have dismissed Adam altogether if I had taken his pride and joy as well as his respectability.

Now I savour Adam's discomfort. I am sorely tempted to bid him cut it off himself, by his own hand – to have it wrapped and sent to the townhouse along with the rest. Instead I smile and I wait. That pleasure shall be saved, perhaps, for a future day, and besides, the smell really would be terrible. I have a position to maintain after all, particularly now that Mr Ashton is dead – of shame, some would say – and everything has fallen to me.

Anyway, I scarcely need go so far. I tap the floor sharply with my cane, the silver-tipped one that had belonged to Millicent's father, and lead the way from the hothouse. This time I go directly to the flowers and shout out my orders, not so very different from those I request every week. Mostly, they are yellow: cyclamen for resignation. Marigolds for cruelty, for grief. A pity it is too late in the year for hyacinths or carnations, though I make a point of asking for them: jealousy, rejection, disappointment, disdain. There is rosemary for simple remembrance – one should have something green – and this time, feeling a little mischievous, I add tiger lilies for wealth and pride. I find I have become somewhat adept at this language that was once his own possession; I rather enjoy slipping in and out of it now and then.

I order everything to be sent to the townhouse, for the pleasure of my wife – he already knows the direction. As he nods and makes some note on a scrap of dirty paper, we both know that it is I who shall enjoy them the most.

~

And she? Ah, but I have taught Millicent a more direct language. Indeed, she has found little use for words as the days of our marriage have worn into weeks; she does not need to tell me what she feels.

Now she is bent over her sewing, engaged as I am, I suppose, on sublime contemplation of this life we have made between us.

I sit back in my armchair with the sigh of a satisfied man. The fire crackles. It shines from the floral arrangement I have placed in the centre of the table – a little strident in its colours, but I like that it cannot be missed, wherever one might sit. My choices arrived prompt to their time, and at my bidding, she unpacked and arranged them in their vase. What were her thoughts, I wonder? But I know what they were. I always know. Adam's messages were obscure, coded, simpering and trite; it is I who taught her the true language of flowers.

Now I breathe in deep and savour their scent and enjoy this, my favourite way to pass an idle hour. I admire Adam's ruin. I look upon Adam's sorrow. I breathe in the scent of Adam's pain.

Suddenly, my dear little wife stands. She looks tired; she looks unhappy. She blinks those luxuriant eyelashes – is there a bead of moisture clinging there? – and she walks from the room, without putting away her sewing, without finishing her tea, without once looking at me or bidding me goodnight.

I reflect that I shall need to teach her better manners.

For now, I push myself from my chair and go to hers and examine her work. She is sewing a patterned border with not a flower or a leaf to be seen. I smile and set it down and sit, for a moment, in her accustomed place. Here she must have rested as a child; here she must have learned at her father's knee, and I suppose her mother's, and listened as they spun tales of what her future would be.

I think of my own mother. I smile fondly. She would have liked my wife, I decide, especially so when she begins to bear fruit. Such a thing can surely not be long in the making. Such a rose! She has lived all her life under a dome of glass and now she lives as in the finest hothouse. Soon, she will begin to bloom.

The fire spits and crackles. It is already as warm as a hothouse, and I reach out for her abandoned cup. The tisane she has made smells faintly of rosemary and I smile before draining it. I drink of her bitterness, and it *is* bitter, and I relish it.

When I stand, I know at once that something is wrong. My lips tingle; my body sways. Perhaps I have taken some chill from my visit to the nursery – that would please her, no doubt. I remain motionless, licking my lips, my senses searching for something – and my gaze rests upon the flowers, for resignation; for grief; for goodbye.

I smile and step towards them, suddenly remembering another bloom on another day: the little pink hybrid I had prepared for her so carefully, ready to present it to her like a page before a queen, only to see it trampled underfoot. That was before she had learned to admire another – but I find myself wondering, for a moment, if we could find a way to be so again. We could be tender; we could put out new shoots, find our way back to each other, twine like stems about one another's hearts.

I shake my head and my vision blurs. I move back, meaning to sit once more, and find myself sprawling full length on the carpet. My head spins and the room with it. Something is *very* wrong.

The teacup has fallen from the table – I must have caught at it with my hand. I stare at the bone china and suddenly wonder: was the teacup full when I drank from it? Had Millicent touched it at all?

I try to call out but only an inarticulate sound emerges, nothing like language, and a cramp doubles me up. I moan; I feel spittle dripping from my lips – or is it foam? There is a great pressure in my chest. I am crying, I realise, like a child. There is something very, *very* wrong, and pain racks me again, rooted in my stomach, something I have eaten perhaps – or something I drank, something close by; something left there on purpose, intended, perhaps, for me.

I open my mouth and thrust my fingers into my throat but instead my jaw clenches and I bite down on them. I cannot make myself vomit; it is inside me, poisonous and deep and very much too late.

I hear little steps, a light foot, the brush of a gown against my leg. I try to focus and make out Millicent standing over me, her posture straight, her countenance calm. As I watch, as if she had come to arrange the *flowers*, for God's sake, she takes hold of the heavy vase and slowly spins it around, though her gaze remains fixed on me, her head tilted as if to better make out my reaction.

And I see it: among the marigolds is something that isn't yellow, that doesn't belong, that I didn't order. I recognise it at once, of course. Not for nothing the years of labour at Petherton's direction, of hanging upon Mr Ashton's coattails. An herbaceous perennial, often cultivated as an ornamental plant, prized for its loveliness, with dark blue flowers that curl like a friar's cowl.

It is monkshood, and it is deadly.

I stare up at her and she stands there and watches me. Soon she is a blur; her eyelashes, her hair, her gown, are nothing but pale fronds, everything curling and swaying beyond my reach. Why did I never suspect that it was she who would teach me a new tongue – a new language of flowers? Perhaps it was always Millicent who understood their meaning better than any of us.

My body is turning entirely numb. I cannot banish the mist drifting over my vision, cannot move my lips, cannot make my feelings heard. But as I stare up at her, I know what it is she means to tell me: that silence is the most perfect language of all.

Also by Alison Littlewood:

Novels
A Cold Season (Jo Fletcher Books, 2011)
Path of Needles (Jo Fletcher Books, 2013)
The Unquiet House (Jo Fletcher Books, 2014)
A Cold Silence (Jo Fletcher Books, 2015)
Acapulcalypse Now (Robinson, 2015)
The Hidden People (Jo Fletcher Books, 2016)
The Crow Garden (Jo Fletcher Books, 2017)
Mistletoe (Jo Fletcher Books, 2019)
The Cottingley Cuckoo (Titan Books, 2021)
     (as by A. J. Elwood)

Novellas
Cottingley (NewCon Press, 2017)

Collections
Five Feathered Tales (Short Scary Tales
Publications, 2016)
Quieter Paths (PS Publishing, 2016)

Now available and forthcoming from
Black Shuck Shadows:

Now available and forthcoming from
Black Shuck Shadows: